Captured By The Pack

The Forbidden Bite By Night

Elle Lacerta

Published by Elle Lacerta, 2023.

This is a work of fiction. Similarities to real people, places, or events are entirely coincidental.

CAPTURED BY THE PACK

First edition. December 11, 2023.

Copyright © 2023 Elle Lacerta.

Written by Elle Lacerta.

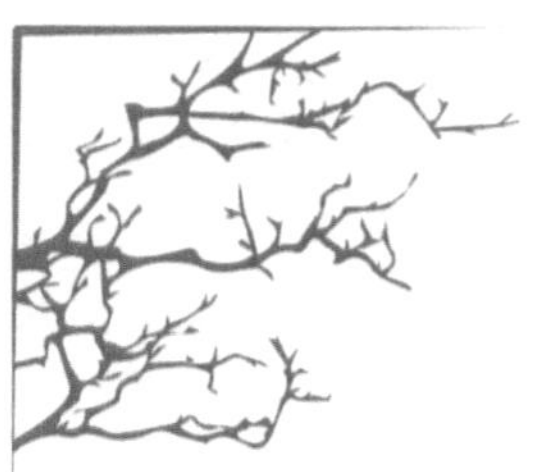

Chapter One

What did she have left to lose?

The sky hung heavy with the crimson hues of dusk as Abigail staggered through the wreckage that was once her hometown. Charred remnants of homes lay scattered, mingling with broken debris that once formed the heart of a bustling village. The distant echoes of chaos still reverberated through the desolation, an empty echo of the tragedy that had befallen her home.

She navigated through the ruins with a heavy heart. In the corner of her eye she caught the sight of the bakery, it's roof caved in, with its stone-bricked oven crumbling beneath the weight of a fallen beam.

Just a few days ago, her sister had been working there. Complaining about her boss breathing down her neck, and the torment of being teased by the baker's son. Just a few days ago, they were talking about going to university, or the pipe dream of going to the Royal Academy-the potential of someday getting a chance to become a Mage.

The thought made her sick.

Rubble crunched beneath her boots as she cautiously made her way past collapsed structures, her gaze sweeping over the destruction.

The once-familiar streets were unrecognizable, the air thick with the acrid scent of smoke and charred wood. Abigail's heart clenched at the sight of her ravaged home, memories of laughter and warmth now replaced by desolation and despair. Tears threatened to spill from her eyes, but she held them at bay, determined to stay composed despite the overwhelming grief that threatened to consume her.

Focus, she repeated in her mind over and over. *Just find Iris, then get Dad, and we get out of Veridian...*

Finding Iris was the first challenge ahead of her. Where were the Caeds keeping her? Was she a servent, maybe forced to bake bread forever for the Prince?

Actually... if that was the case, there were worse fates she could think of.

No, Iris was never *that* lucky.

Maybe she would be tending to the gardens. The days would be long, but she'd enjoy it a little, at least. She'd take after their mother, who had spent every waking moment amongst the flowers and the fields, seeking an escape from the darkness that brewed within the city streets.

As she rounded a corner, her eyes fell upon a lone figure amidst the rubble. A magnificent horse, its coat the deepest shade of midnight black, stood tall and proud. The beast's regal demeanor stood in stark contrast to the destruction surrounding it. Abigail's gaze lingered on the horse's form, noticing the intricate crest emblazoned on its saddle- a symbol she knew all too well.

The gold crest- depicting a bleeding bat- was boldly presented, glistening in the waning light.

"The Caeds," she murmured under her breath, recognizing the emblem of the powerful vampire dynasty that had long held dominion over the lands. It was a mark of prestige and power, reserved for those in the highest echelons of the Caed hierarchy.

Approaching cautiously, Abigail noted the remnants of magical runes etched into the ground nearby, evidence of a fierce struggle that had taken place. Her eyes scanned the area, searching for any signs of life amidst the ruins. But there was just silence, broken only by the occasional howl of the wind.

The horse regarded her with intelligent eyes, its gaze unwavering yet tinged with a sense of weariness. It bore no visible injuries, an unlikely beacon strength and resilience amidst the chaos. Abigail approached slowly, her movements measured, not wanting to startle the majestic creature.

She extended a hand, offering a reassuring gesture as she spoke in a soft, soothing tone.

"Easy there, friend. I mean you no harm."

The horse regarded her for a moment, as if weighing her intentions, before taking a tentative step forward. Its movements were graceful, a testament to its training and discipline. Gently, she reached out, running her hand along the horse's sleek, ebony mane. The animal seemed to lean into her touch, a silent acknowledgement of her presence.

With the village in ruins and her former life shattered, she knew she couldn't stay. But the sight of the horse, bearing the mark of the Caeds, presented an opportunity- a chance to seek answers, to unravel the mystery behind the devastation that had befallen her home.

With a determined resolve, Abigail mounted the horse, settling into the saddle. The animal responded to her touch, its movements fluid and responsive. With a gentle nudge of her heels, they set off, leaving behind the remnants of a the world she had known.

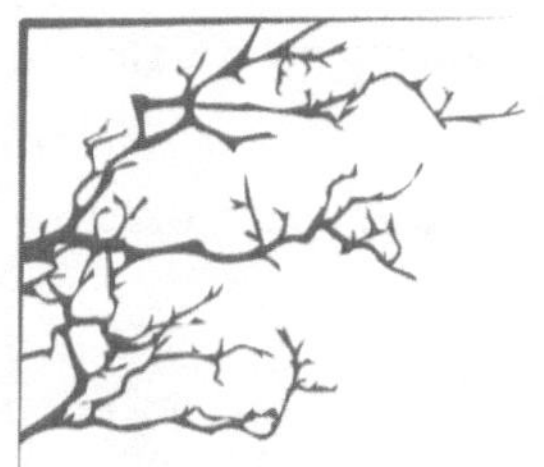

Chapter Two

The night enveloped the land in a cloak of obsidian, a myriad of stars twinkling like scattered diamonds in the vast expanse above.

Abigail urged her steed onward, the horse's breath misting in the chill of the night air as they traversed the uneven terrain. The Caedwyn castle loomed like a menacing specter on the horizon, its towering spires piercing the darkness, a haunting silhouette against the sky.

She had to get to it soon- her sister Iris surely suffered every moment she spent imprisoned within those formidable walls.

Pausing on the outskirts of the castle grounds, Abigail surveyed the foreboding structure with a furrowed brow. The castle's imposing presence seemed impenetrable, its walls standing as a formidable barrier to her quest. But the flicker of determination in her eyes burned brighter, igniting a resolve to rescue Iris and unearth the truth shrouded within the castle's depths.

Before venturing further, Abigail knew she needed a weapon- a means to protect herself against the unknown perils lurking within the castle's confines. Scanning the horizon, a distant glimmer caught her attention, a faint beacon in the dark void ahead.

Everyone in Veridian and the Fyrean kingdom beyond knew the cost of innocence. The cost that those who were too naive, too pure against the harsh reality that the reign of vampires had imposed upon them, a price for the protection of the mages so intertwined with the monsters above them.

She'd need something *strong*.

No normal sword would do.

Weapons capable of killing vampires had long since been banned by the Caeds, but those who had dipped their toes in the forbidden waters of Arcane magic knew that they were out there. Just out of reach of the peasant humans who would have enough spite to wield them.

But oh, she had *plenty* of spite to spare.

With a determined grip on the reins, Abigail guided her horse toward the distant glow. The journey was arduous, navigating through rugged terrain and winding paths. Hours passed before the outline of a town emerged, its faint lights shimmering in the distance like twinkling stars in the night sky.

As she approached the town, Abigail sensed the palpable desolation that hung heavy in the air- a stark contrast to the lively ambiance she once knew back home. The streets, once bustling with life, now lay eerily deserted, buildings standing as silent witnesses to abandonment and neglect. Undeterred by the eerie silence, Abigail pressed forward.

Dismounting from her horse, she secured the reins before venturing into the forsaken town. Her footsteps echoed through the cobblestone streets, the sound reverberating against the hollow facades of the buildings.

Abigail scoured the abandoned streets, her keen eyes searching for any sign of life or hope. Amidst the dilapidated storefronts, a weathered sign caught her eye- an emblem depicting a hammer and anvil, marking a blacksmith's workshop.

Surely there would be a weapon there. It might not be what I'm looking for, but I'd rather have something pointy than becoming another damsel in distress.

Approaching the workshop with cautious steps, Abigail pushed open the creaking door, revealing the interior in disarray. Pushing the creaking door open, Abigail cautiously stepped inside. The forge lay dormant, its embers long extinguished. Tools laid scattered haphazardly throughout the room. The silence of the abandoned workshop hung heavy in the air, broken only by the sound of her own footsteps on the dusty floorboards.

Her eyes caught something bronze within the rubble. She leaned down, her fingers warm against the icy metal pole. Shaking it loose from the debris, she held up the shining metal poker, once meant to stoke the forge's fire.

Well, it's pointy.

It would do, for now.

A sudden loud creak made her jump. She ducked behind the table in front of the forge, her small stature tucked neatly beneath the stone edge, the metal poker clutched tightly in her hand.

A pair of boys entered, all around her age, if not a little older. One with a mess of ginger curls, freckle-dappled cheeks, and a set of light chainmail armor entered the workshop first, his golden eyes wide with apprehension. He was tall, and despite the fact that he was well built and clearly could handle himself, he had this nervous air about him- fidgeting like a uneasy puppy.

"I-I don't feel right about this, Tamsen," he muttered, glancing around the dimly lit space.

Following closely behind was apparently Tamsen, exuding confidence in his tall, athletic stature. His blond hair catching the faint light that filtered through the dusty windows, he moved with a confident stride. His blue eyes darted around the disordered space, sharp and observant.

"Mages," he muttered, his voice edged with tension. "I can smell them. Stay alert."

Abigail's heart raced as she listened to their conversation, weighing her options. She recognized Simon's unease and Tamsen's vigilant demeanor. This could be her chance to seek help, despite the risks.

Or, they could turn on her.

Attack her, or worse...

Sell her to the Crown.

No.

She wasn't going to end up like Iris.

Summoning her courage, Abigail emerged from her hiding spot, brandishing the metal poker and lunging towards Simon. The metal poker connected with a resounding clang against Simon's shoulder, causing him to stagger back with a pained yelp.

Reacting instantly, Tamsen sprang into action, swiftly closing the gap between them. With agility and precision, he intercepted Abigail's strike, seizing her wrist before she could make another move. His grip was firm, yet surprisingly gentle.

"What madness is this?!" Tamsen demanded, his voice almost a bellow as he locked eyes with Abigail, clashing in a tense standoff.

Struggling against his hold, Abigail met his piercing gaze.

"I-I need your help," she gasped, desperation and determination mingling in her voice.

"Why attack us then?" Tamsen's tone remained stern, but a hint of curiosity flickered in his eyes. "A rather impolite way of asking for help, that's for damn sure."

With a rush of urgency, Abigail blurted out, "My sister, she's been taken by the Caeds."

Tamsen's grip relaxed slightly, understanding dawning in his expression.

"Caeds," he echoed, his voice softening. "I might know someone who can assist you."

Simon, rubbing his shoulder and recovering from the surprise attack, glanced between them, concern etched on his face as he listened intently.

Tamsen released Abigail's wrist, stepping back to give her space. His eyes narrowed in contemplation as he assessed her, the urgency in her plea not lost on him.

"The Caeds aren't to be underestimated. Why are they after your sister?" His voice held a note of concern, his natural leadership coming to the forefront.

"I don't know," she confessed. "I really don't."

Simon, still nursing his shoulder and observing the interaction between Tamsen and Abigail, spoke up hesitantly.

"T-Tamsen, we can't get involved in this. It's dangerous. .."

"We can't turn a blind eye, Simon," Tamsen asserted firmly, his attention shifting back to Abigail. "We have connections that might be of use to you, at least."

Simon shifted uncomfortably, torn between his loyalty to Tamsen and his concern for the potential risks.

"But what about Naomi?" he interjected. "We have our own priorities to-"

"Quiet for a moment," The taller male snapped, frustration edging his tone. He lowered his voice to a whisper. "I might know someone that could help you get your hands on an Arcane blade, if that will keep you from bonking my friend again."

"An Arcane blade, you say?" She said, raising an eyebrow skeptically. "Fine, I'll spare him."

"There's a traveler, a shady sort," Tamsen continued, a faint smile on his lips. "Goes by Jett. He deals in forbidden weapons. Sells 'em to those desperate enough to seek 'em. Dangerous things, they are. He's been seen at the edge of town."

Forbidden weapons were not to be trifled with, yet her determination to rescue her sister spurred her on.

"Where can I find him?"

After a moment, he pointed towards the outskirts of the town. "Head east, towards the old abandoned mill. The tavern across the street is still standing. He's been seen skulking around there."

"Thanks," She smiled, breathing a sigh of relief. She couldn't believe that things hadn't taken a turn, and with the prospects of a forbidden weapon on the horizen- she held her chin high as she left the workshop. Mounting her horse once more, she rode toward the outskirts, the revelation of a shady traveler dealing in Arcane weapons adding a new layer of complexity to her mission.

"You think that was a good idea?"

"When did I say I had good ideas?" Tamsen retorted as he twirled the metal poker between his fingers. Soot stuck beneath his nails, caking into the threads of his shirt, a bitter reminder of the task at hand. "She thinks she's got this. She'll learn the hard way, but that's not our problem."

The two worked to finish looting the ruins. A few coppers had been scattered amongst the rubble, but not much more. The little brat had probably picked it clean first. Either way, it meant another fruitless run, and another waste of time.

"T-they won't..." Simon trailed off, picking at the hem of his sleeve. "They won't just...k-kill her..."

"No," Tamsen agreed. "They won't."

"D-do you think..." Simon swallowed hard, the words almost making him sick.

There was so many things they could do to her.

So many things they would.

"There's no point in thinking about it," Tamsen interrupted. He ran a hand through his hair as the two stepped back out onto the cobblestone street, a chill breeze biting through the evening air. "Don't start down that road. She thinks she's a strong, independant girl. There's no wrangling that, bucko."

Simon opened his mouth to speak, but he couldn't seem to find a reply.

"Come on," Tamsen said, clasping an arm around his shoulder, forgetting about the injury until Simon yelped. "Ah- sorry. Cheer up, we've got work ahead of us. Let's go back to camp and figure out how we're going to gut those bloody vampires."

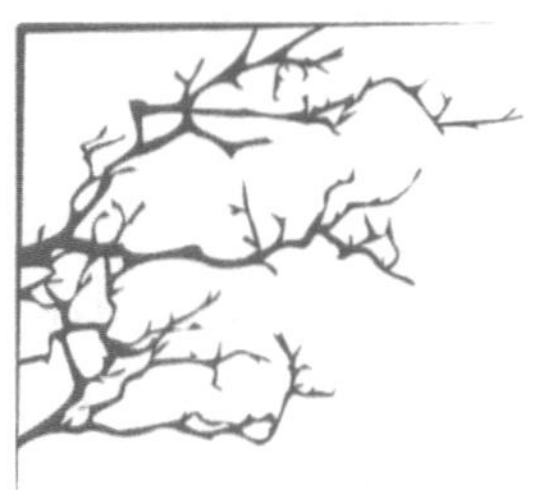

Chapter Three

The moon, a glistening orb in the night sky, cast its ethereal glow over the dense canopy of the forest. Abbie gripped the reins of the stolen horse, its hooves pounding against the damp earth, echoing the urgency pulsating within her. The mission to rescue Iris drove her forward, eclipsing the fear that threatened to consume her.

The city sprawled ahead, its looming silhouette dominated by the imposing walls of the castle. Abbie knew she couldn't confront the fortress alone. She needed a weapon, and maybe the help of someone adept at navigating through heavily guarded domains. Rumors had hinted at a shadowy traveler who peddled more than just wares.

With determination etched into every step, Abbie traversed the winding streets until she found herself amidst the underbelly of the city. Her relentless pursuit guided her to a dilapidated tavern, its time-worn doors groaning in protest as she nudged them open, allowing dim light to spill into the shadowed expanse within

Inside, the tavern's ambiance spoke of a bygone era, the low-hanging haze mingling with the scent of aged wood and stale ale. Shadows danced and swirled in the corners, shrouding secluded alcoves and worn tables that bore the marks of countless years of use. The flickering candlelight cast an eerie yet mesmerizing glow, illuminating patches of weathered walls adorned with cracked tapestries and faded paintings, telling tales of forgotten heroes and lost causes.

Amidst this scene, a lone figure sat ensconced in the farthest recesses of the tavern. The man cut a striking figure- a mantle of midnight-black hair framing a brooding countenance. His angular features were cast in the dim light, revealing a chiseled jawline beneath the shadow of a furrowed brow. Chestnut eyes, akin to polished mahogany, held a glint of detached curiosity as they surveyed the comings and goings within the establishment.

A weathered leather jerkin adorned his frame, a testament to battles both won and yet to be fought. The fabric of his shirt bore the faint remnants of a once-rich hue, now faded by time and a life spent in the shadows. Adorned with an array of belts, each buckle held an assortment of small pouches concealing the secrets of his trade- a collection of trinkets and tools that hinted at his expertise in weaponry.

Approaching his table, Abbie masked her apprehension as best she could.

"Are you Jett?"

A smirk danced across his lips.

"Depends. Who's asking?"

"I need a weapon," she stated bluntly, her voice steady despite the racing of her heart. "And I need someone who can help me infiltrate the castle."

Jett's gaze lingered on her, assessing her determination.

"That's a tall order, Darling. What's in it for me?"

"I can pay," she replied, revealing a pouch of coins from her bag. "And I offer my assistance in return."

"Assistance, you say? Intriguing. But storming that castle won't come cheap. What are you willing to give?"

"Anything," Abbie declared, her voice resolute.

"Are you sure about that?" He leaned in, closing the gap between them.

He smelled like a mix of sweet summer cherries and smooth leather. His eyes- the deepest, murkiest pools she had ever seen- filled with a deadly combination of amusement and malice.

"C-certain," She replied, looking away as a slight blush crept across her cheeks.

"Very well then. We have a deal. But make no mistake- I don't do charity, and I don't do strings attached."

OUTSIDE THE TAVERN, the night air crackled with a sense of secrecy, carrying whispers of clandestine deals and hidden motives. Abbie fell into step beside Jett, traversing narrow alleys and deserted streets, the moon's luminescence painting a silvered path before them.

They arrived at a secluded alcove, and from beneath his cloak, Jett produced an array of gleaming blades, each whispering tales of deadly elegance.

"Take your pick, darling. Choose wisely."

Abbie's gaze danced over the weapons, her fingers delicately tracing the lethal edges before settling on a slender dagger with an ornate hilt- an exquisite marriage of beauty and lethality.

"A fine choice," Jett remarked, a hint of approval coloring his voice. "Now, onto our next move..."

Before he could continue, a sudden commotion erupted nearby- the patrol of city guards, their torches illuminating the night as they swept through the area. Panic seized Abbie's chest, her heartbeat drumming a frenzied rhythm.

Reacting swiftly, Jett seized her arm, pulling her into the recesses of the shadows. Their bodies pressed close together in the cramped space, sending an unexpected surge of heat through her despite the chill of the night.

For an agonizing moment, they remained concealed, their breaths suspended as the sounds of the guards' footsteps faded into the distance. As the danger passed, Jett released her, a sly grin playing on his lips.

"Looks like we're in for quite the adventure, Darling. Ready to breach a castle?"

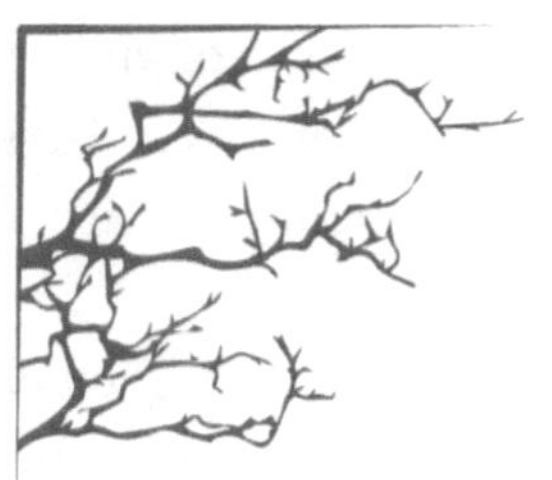

Chapter Four

As the echoes of the retreating guards faded into the night, Abbie's breaths came in ragged gasps, adrenaline still coursing through her veins. She straightened herself, trying to regain composure, while Jett leaned against the weathered brick wall, a wry grin etched upon his face.

"Seems like we gave them the slip," he remarked, his voice a low murmur, his eyes glinting with a playful edge.

Abbie sighed as the rush of relief flooded her.

"Thank you for that. I wouldn't have-"

"Shh," Jett interrupted, a finger pressed against her lips as he cast a cautious glance around. "We're not out of the woods yet, Darling. But we should get moving."

With a subtle nod, Abbie followed as Jett led her through a maze of back alleys and hidden passages, each step carefully calculated to evade the ever-watchful eye of the city's guards. Shadows clung to the cobblestones, their movements stealthy, as if the night itself conspired to conceal their presence.

As they emerged from the labyrinthine streets, a secluded clearing came into view, bathed in the gentle glow of a crackling fire. Tents were pitched haphazardly, casting elongated shadows that danced against the trees. A small group of individuals lounged around the fire, their laughter mingling with the crackling flames.

Jett gestured towards the makeshift camp. "Welcome to our humble abode, Darling. We're camping here to keep out of the Crown's prying eyes, but we're moving again in the morning."

The crackling fire painted the clearing in flickering hues of amber and gold, casting dancing shadows upon the surrounding trees. Two figures- *unfortunately familiar ones-* sat by the flames, their presence a study in contrasts against the serene backdrop of the campsite.

"Ah, hello again, poker girl," Tamsen replied with a passing glance, paying little attention to the newcomer. "Back for another round in the ring with Simon?"

"Piss off," The redhead mumbled.

Tamsen picked up a tiny stone, aiming right for Jett. Had he not made a quick side-step, he would've been pebble-pelted square in the nose.

"You should've mentioned you were busy chasing tail again, Jett. Simon and I were waiting for you all damn day."

"Oh, please," Jett replied with a roll of his eyes. "I was pawning off a few extra trinkets at the village. She wants to come along for the big sha-bang."

Simon, with his average stature and a mop of curly red hair, sat hunched over a worn leather-bound book, golden eyes flitting across the pages. His fingers traced the words delicately, lost in the world of ancient texts and forgotten lore. Nervous energy hummed around him like a quiet melody, and his gaze flicked from Tamsen to the darkened forest's edge.

"J-join us?" He bit his lip, lowering his voice. "But she's...not..."

"It's fine," Jett interjected. "I'm sure Tamsen will find a use for her."

"Your name?" Opposite him sat Tamsen, an imposing figure with blonde hair tousled by the evening breeze, his piercing blue eyes scanning the surroundings with a predatory focus. Tall and athletic, he exuded an aura of dominance and quiet authority, every movement steeped in an innate sense of leadership.

"Abigail. You can call me Abbie."

"Just don't get in the way, *Abbie*," He grumbled, running a hand through his hair. "I can get in there myself if I have to, but I'm not going to be your savior if you get yourself caught."

"Never asked you to," Abbie asserted. "I just want to find my sister and get the hell out of here, get as far away from the castle as we can possibly get..."

"I-I'm looking for my sister, too," Simon murmured. "She disappeared some time ago. I think...I think they would have taken her there, if they..."

Simon's breath hitched, but he didn't dare continue. Tamsen's expression darkened at the mention of the castle. The flames danced in his eyes, reflecting a simmering resentment.

"The castle... a place of darkness and deceit. Each of us bears a reason to despise it."

She sat down with them on the soft, mossy ground below, basking in the warm glow of the fire. For the first time since she had found the note from their father, she felt the tension slip from her, finally allowing herself to ease.

They look more than capable. They seem friendly. And, one of them so happened to have an arsenal of Arcane weapons- just the type of person that someone with a grudge against vampires would die to meet.

Abbie broke the silence, her voice soft but resolute.

"Thank you for helping me, all of you."

Tamsen's gaze softened briefly, a hint of something vulnerable flickering in his eyes before his facade of dominance returned.

"We all have our reasons for being here. Whatever your quest may be, Abigail, know that you're not alone in this endeavor."

Simon nodded in agreement, a tentative smile forming on his lips. "We'll help however we can."

The words hung in the air, a promise of camaraderie and solidarity in the face of adversity. For the first time, the weight of her task seemed less daunting, and the road ahead appeared less bleak. Perhaps, in this ragtag group of misfits, she had finally found her people.

"So, how'd you three end up planning to siege a castle?" Abbie asked curiously as the moon rose above.

Simon spoke up. "I'm the Beta, and one of the pack members. Tamsen's an Alpha, and so is Jett. Tamsen wants the throne. Jett just wants his mother back."

Pack...?

Abigail's eyes widened.

No. I must have heard them wrong.

But the words swirled around her mind like the smoke in the summer night-

Beta. Alpha. Pack.

That only meant one thing.

Werewolves.

"That's... a lot to bear," Abbie said softly, her gaze shifting from Simon to Tamsen and Jett, a newfound understanding coloring her perception of the trio.

She shifted slightly, drawing her knees closer to her chest, the warmth of the fire not quite enough to dispel the chill that crept into her bones. However, it wasn't just the night's cold that sent shivers down her spine; it was the realization that the people she'd have to trust and rely on weren't just outcasts in the eyes of society, they were something far more perilous.

"Your mother?" Abbie questioned.

"My mother was taken from me, and the only lead I have is the castle. So, I'm joining this little escapade."

"What about you?" Abbie asked Simon. "You said you're looking for your sister. What happened?"

Simon bit his lip, glancing away. "Well, it's not a very long story, actually. My sister... she's always been more outgoing than me. One day, she said she was going into town, and that was the last I saw of her."

"Do you know why they would have taken her?"

"She wanted to train as a mage, even though we were forbidden from entering the kingdom... I think she was taken because her power.."

"And you're a shifter, right?"

Simon nodded, his expression becoming downcast. "Yes, and my sister was, too. She was taken a long time ago. I was really young, and I was taken care of by the pack, but I'd still like to see her again."

"I understand," Abbie said, her voice soft. "I'm sorry."

"It's alright," Simon replied, a weak smile playing on his lips. "I'll find her someday."

"We'll find them both, and bring them home," Tamsen said.

A brief silence passed, each of them lost in their own thoughts.

"I've always been a believer that those who challenge the norm are often the ones who shape the world," Abbie offered, her tone measured yet carrying a tinge of understanding. "But there's a difference between bending the rules and breaking them."

She glanced around the campfire, meeting each of their gazes in turn. Simon's eyes held a glimmer of hope tinged with sadness, Tamsen's a quiet determination, and Jett's a mix of pain and resolve. But there was something more lurking beneath the surface, something Abbie couldn't quite put her finger on.

"The difference is always shifting, because they constantly change the rules at be. There's no winning their game."

AS THE CONVERSATION drifted to lighter subjects, Abbie's mind whirled with questions and apprehensions. She masked her shock well, concealing the revelation that they were werewolves- creatures the empire had long deemed enemies to be eradicated on sight.

"So, what's your sister like, Abbie?" Simon asked.

"She's a bit younger than me, but she's very headstrong. She can get into trouble sometimes, but she always has a good heart. Her name's Iris...I miss her."

"Iris," Simon repeated. "She's a lucky girl to have a sister like you."

Abbie smiled. "Thank you. I'm glad I met you all. I don't know how I'd be able to do this on my own."

"Don't worry, Darling. You won't have to," Jett purred, giving her a wink.

Tamsen observed the exchange, a glint of curiosity dancing in his eyes before he leaned back, feigning disinterest as he stared into the depths of the fire. The flickering flames seemed to mirror the subtle tension lingering among them.

Abbie felt the familiar warmth rising in her cheeks, and she glanced away, hoping that the firelight would conceal the blush.

"I hope so," she murmured, a faint smile playing on her lips.

The flames ate away at the logs beneath, time fading in gentle camaraderie. Simon and Jett, engrossed in a conversation about the best way to craft a sword hilt, barely noticed the subtle shift in Tamsen's demeanor as he turned slightly toward Abigail. His gaze held a curious warmth as he broached a more personal subject.

"You're sure you want to risk this? Isn't there someone waiting for you back home?" Tamsen's voice held a gentle inquisitiveness, his eyes reflecting the flickering flames.

Abigail glanced toward the dark horizon, contemplating her response. A soft sigh escaped her lips, almost lost amidst the night's whispers.

"No," she began, choosing her words with care. "It's not that simple."

"It's not common that I don't have to fight someone for something so beautiful," He remarked, a playful attempt at lightening things, but it didn't seem to sink in. Abbie's eyes were distant, a sea of sadness, loss and longing.

She toyed with a twig, tracing invisible patterns in the dirt before continuing. "The mage's health examinations... they've made it difficult for me to consider anything serious. It's complicated."

Tamsen bristled at her response.

It was all so normal for humans.

The way things worked, the way they obeyed whatever the bloodsuckers wanted- even going so far as to volunteer as the perfect bloodslave for the monsters. Often times, a baron, or even a Prince would visit a village in the Fyrean kingdom, round up the girls who had come of age- taken them under the guise that a well-fed life as livestock is better than a lowly beggar.

Of course they'd only want the finest bloodbags.

So, in addition to keeping werewolves from entering the kingdom's sacred ground, every year a handful of skilled Mages would examine the quality of the food- or rather, testing them for any ailments or abnormalities, assuring only the best for the vampires who reigned.

Despite wanting to ask more, Tamsen nodded, understanding flickering in his eyes. Instead, he offered a reassuring smile, a silent acknowledgment of her unspoken burden.

"You wouldn't know anything of the Arcane, would you?" Tamsen asked, eager to change the subject. "Could be useful, y'know."

"N-No," Abbie replied, shaking her head. "Just some minor training in reading runes, but... I didn't pay attention that well. Most of the tutoring sessions I spent with my nose in my sketchbook."

"We can teach you," Tamsen replied. "It would be our pleasure."

"If you'll have me," Abbie replied.

Tamsen flashed her a wolfish grin, his gaze darkening.

"Of course, *Sugar*. We'll always have a place for you."

THE DAY'S TRAVELS HAD left Abbie fatigued, her muscles aching with each movement as the night settled around them, painting the sky in shades of indigo and obsidian. The campsite was enveloped in an eerie calmness, save for the crackling remnants of the fire, casting fleeting shadows that danced across the ground.

"It's gonna start getting cold out soon," Jett's smooth voice purred. "You can take my tent, Darling. I'll keep watch."

"Like hell she will," Tamsen snapped. "She'll stay with me."

Jett arched a brow. "Really? Are you sure about that, big guy?"

"Quite," Tamsen responded, a low growl underpinning his words, a subtle smirk playing on his lips. "Come on, Abbie. It's late."

"I think I might stay up a little longer."

Simon's gaze flickered between the two of them, his expression unreadable. "Are you sure? It's not safe to wander alone at night."

"I'll be fine, I'm just...nervous. I think I'll draw for a bit," Her voice carried a hint of determination, her fingers itching for the solace found within the strokes of her sketches. "Thank you Jett, and thank you Tamsen- but I'm good."

The conversation lingered in the air, a subtle tension seemed to crackle within the circle, the unspoken dynamics among them shifting with the revelation of Tamsen's protective stance. Despite his initially assertive tone, there was an underlying layer of care in his insistence, a hint of a primal instinct.

"You...sure?"

"Certain. Thanks, Tamsen."

As Simon nodded, conceding to her choice, Tamsen's expression darkened imperceptibly, the glint of his Alpha side peeking through the facade of calm. However, he refrained from pressing further, his gaze lingering on Abbie for a moment longer before he turned away, his posture rigid with contained tension.

"Well, if you're certain. Don't say I didn't warn you," Simon replied, closing the book in his lap.

Abbie nodded, offering him a small smile. "Thanks. I appreciate it."

As the others retired for the evening, Abbie settled herself by the dying embers of the fire, although Simon stayed back with her. He was the youngest and timidest, yet he seemed the most concerned.

She gave a faint acknowledging glance toward Tamsen, then she settled herself by the fire, her sketchbook and charcoal becoming her companions in the quiet hours of the night. As the others retreated to their respective shelters, the shadows lengthened, and Abbie found herself immersed in the rhythmic motion of her art

"It's okay, I'll be fine. You should get some rest," Abbie said, reaching out to touch his hand.

Simon looked up at her, his gaze meeting hers. For a moment, Abbie felt a flicker of warmth, an undercurrent of desire.

"I know. I just wanted to make sure you're okay. It's dangerous out here, especially for a human."

Underneath the canopy of stars, the campfire's fading embers painted the clearing in a soft, muted glow. Simon and Abbie lingered by the dying flames, a subtle tension hanging between them as they exchanged hesitant glances, both seemingly caught in the unspoken pull of a budding connection.

"Abbie," Simon began tentatively, his voice soft amidst the nighttime hush. "We... we only have three tents. I'm afraid there might not be enough room for everyone."

"Oh, I didn't consider that..." Her eyes fell to the flames, and she bit the inside of her cheek. After a moment of hesitation, she continued. "I can sleep outside. I don't want to impose."

Simon's nerves prickled, his heart pounding with an unexpected boldness.

"I-I could... I mean, if you'd like, you could share my tent. I don't mind sleeping outside if it makes you more comfortable around the others."

Abbie's gaze met Simon's, a mixture of gratitude and uncertainty flashing in her eyes. "That's really kind of you, Simon. But I don't want to intrude."

Simon swallowed hard, mustering the courage to reassure her. "You wouldn't be intruding. It's just... I wouldn't want you to feel awkward around the others. They can be... a bit much sometimes."

She hesitated, deliberating his offer before finally nodding with a soft smile.

"Thank you, Simon. I appreciate it."

He led Abbie to his tent, the soft glow of the lantern illuminating the cozy interior. The air was scented with pine and a hint of smoke, the warmth of the blankets inviting against the cool night breeze.

"I'll... I'll sleep outside," Simon offered hesitantly, gesturing toward the open flap of the tent. "You can have the bed. It's more comfortable."

"Thank you, Simon. But I couldn't let you do that. It's your tent, after all."

Simon paused, his heart racing as he battled with his nerves. "I-I insist. It's... it's the least I can do. Please, I want you to be comfortable."

"Simon-"

Simon hesitated for a moment before clearing his throat, his voice tinged with a touch of bashfulness. "Would you like... to share the bed?"

Abbie glanced around the tent, a shy smile playing on her lips.

"Sure, if that's alright with you."

Simon nodded, trying to suppress the rapid beating of his heart as they settled onto the bed, the warmth of their proximity creating an electric charge that crackled between them. He lay down first, carefully leaving space for Abbie, who nestled herself beside him, her presence bringing a sense of comfort that he hadn't anticipated.

The shared space was cozy, their bodies mere inches apart, yet a vast ocean of unspoken feelings and uncharted territory lay between them. Simon's nerves danced like fireflies in the night, his breaths shallow as he felt the brush of Abbie's warmth against his side.

The air seemed to hum with a soft intimacy, a fragile tenderness enveloping them in a cocoon of quietude. Simon glanced down, his heart skipping a beat as their eyes met, the faint light casting a soft radiance upon Abbie's features, highlighting the delicate curve of her cheek, the gentle flutter of her lashes against her skin.

"I've never done this with a girl," He said, his confession a shy whisper.

In a moment of unspoken understanding, Abbie shifted closer, her head resting gently against Simon's chest, their bodies fitting together as if they were two pieces of a puzzle finding their perfect match. His heartbeat quickened at the closeness, the rhythmic thud echoing in the quiet space between them.

"Well, you're not bad at it."

Simon wrapped an arm around Abbie, his touch gentle yet possessive, a protective instinct surging within him as he pulled her closer. Their breaths mingled in the stillness of the night, each exhale a whispered symphony that spoke volumes in the language of unspoken emotions.

"N-neither are you," He said, feeling the heat rise in his cheeks.

"Simon," she murmured, her voice barely above a whisper, "I know how hard it can be... what you're going through. I promise, I'll help you find your sister. We'll search together until we find her."

Simon met her gaze, his heart swelling with a mixture of gratitude and determination. He tightened his embrace, a gentle warmth enveloping Abbie as he spoke with conviction.

"And I promise you, Abbie," he murmured, his voice laced with sincerity, "I'll do everything in my power to help you rescue Iris from that castle. We're in this together. You can count on me."

The warmth of their bodies melding together, their closeness sparking an unforeseen flame that flickered in the tender intimacy of the moment.

As sleep began to gently claim them, they lay intertwined in a silent embrace, the uncharted territory of their connection unfolding beneath the starlit sky- a delicate dance of hearts finding solace and a sense of belonging in each other's presence.

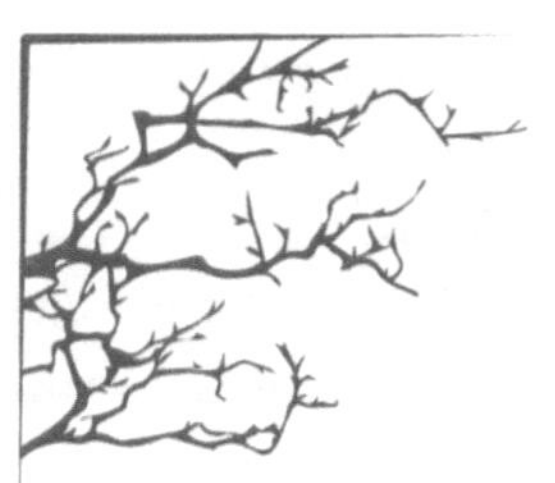

Chapter Five

A bbie's heart raced as the boy led her into the barn, the scent of fresh hay and weathered wood filling her senses.

"Are we allowed in here?" she asked, her voice timid as her freckle-laden cheeks reddened, her eyes glancing anxiously around the barn. They were alone, at least- no sounds other than the soft jingle of the horses' tackle mounted on the wall as a breeze swept through the barn doors. They were alone, even the stallions out training with their riders, leaving the intimate space only for them.

"Well, do you plan on telling anyone?"

The boy, whose name Abbie couldn't remember, had been flirting with her the whole night while she volunteered a shift at the bakery to cover for Iris, and she had to admit- he was very cute. He was the first boy she'd seen in ages who made her heart jump like this.

He led her behind a pile of hay and sat her down. She couldn't meet his gaze, her heart threatening to thump out of her chest. To keep herself from fidgeting, Abbie sat on her hands and looked at the floor as the boy leaned into her. He pressed his lips to hers and kissed her gently. Abbie's pulse raced and she was unsure of what to do.

Her first kiss.

She had seen the other village girls make out with their boyfriends, but she had no idea what to actually do.

Abigail opened her eyes, but instead of the murky blue eyes, sharp nose, and dirt-splattered shirt of the farmer's boy she'd chosen on a whim, she saw the gold-speckled eyes of Simon, red wisps of hair framing his freck-led cheeks. His mouth was on hers, and it felt good. The warmth spread *throughout her body, and she felt like a million butterflies were exploding inside her.*

His lips were soft, and the scruff on his chin scratched her face in the most delectable way. It was a new sensation, a new feeling, and it was exciting. She could feel the heat radiating off his body as he wrapped his arms around her, and she pulled him close, wanting to feel his body against hers.

He laid her down on the soft hay and continued to kiss her. She ran her fingers through his hair and enjoyed the sensation of his lips on hers. It was the best feeling in the world, and she wanted more.

She could feel the bulge in his pants pressing against her, and it made her nervous, but she didn't want him to stop.

Simon broke the kiss and stared at her.

"You're so beautiful."

Abbie blushed. She wasn't used to compliments. In fact, she'd never had a boy say that to her before. She smiled and kissed him again, this time, taking the lead. She let her fingers graze over his smooth skin, taking a deep breath of his scent. The scent of pine and hay lingered, and she buried her face into his neck. His hand wandered up her shirt and cupped her breast.

Fuck...

She could barely think, arching into him. Then, when she realized how exposed she was, her eyes widened and she pulled away.

"What's wrong?" he asked.

"Nothing. I just... I'm not sure about this."

He pulled her close and kissed her neck.

"Don't worry. I'll be gentle, and if you want me to stop, I'll do it in a heartbeat."

"Okay," She said, offering a smile. "I trust you."

He slipped his hand under her shirt and cupped her breast again. This time, she didn't pull away. She let him fondle her for a few minutes before he pulled her dress over her head, along with the flour-caked apron she'd worn for the day, tossing it to the dusty, hay-laden floorboards below.

Her heart skipped a beat as the fleeting panic of a nagging thought crept its way in-

Is he going to say something about the scar?

She shivered, goosebumps erupting over her skin. She tried not to feel embarrassed. She had always been self-conscious about her body, and she feared Simon wouldn't approve.

But instead, he let out a hungry sigh, kissing her chest, down to her stomach, her skin quivering beneath the warmth.

"You're so beautiful," he said.

"Thanks," she replied with a breath of relief, trying to hide her blush.

He pulled her close and kissed her, his tongue exploring her mouth.

She moaned as his hands roamed over her body. It felt good, and she could feel her excitement growing.

He slid his hand down her pants and rubbed her clit through the fabric of her underwear. She gasped and arched her back, pushing against his hand. It felt so good, and she wanted more. She kissed him and slid her hand down to his pants, rubbing his bulge through the fabric. He moaned and fumbled to unbutton his pants, pulling his hard cock out.

She bit her lip and reached for his cock, wrapping her fingers around the thick shaft. He rubbed her clit, and she stroked his cock, both of them moaning in pleasure.

He kissed her neck and nibbled on her earlobe.

She was getting close. She could feel the familiar sensation building within her. The same thing she'd felt every night when she pleasured herself, but this was so much better.

"That feels so good," she whispered.

"I know," he replied, his breath hot against her ear.

"I want you."

"Me, too."

He slid her panties down her legs, revealing her naked form to the moonlight-

THE NEXT MORNING, WHEN Abbie awoke with a jolt, she was alone.

As the sun filtered through the canvas walls of the tent, she rubbed the sleep from her eyes and sat up, stretching the stiffness from her limbs. She glanced around, realizing she'd been wrapped up in Simon's bedroll, a faint trace of his scent still lingering on the blankets.

A soft smile tugged at the corners of her lips, a subtle blush warming her cheeks. The night had brought them closer, and in the soft hush of the morning, she found herself wondering what would happen between them. Clearly, he hadn't tried to make a move, so he wasn't in it just for a one night escapade- unlike the boys she'd had before.

She dressed quickly, smoothing her clothes and hair before exiting the tent. Simon and Tamsen stood by the smoldering remains of last night's campfire, their hushed voices drifting in the breeze.

Simon glanced at her, then, when Tamsen was distracted by her sudden appearance, he mouthed the words:

I slept outside, got it?

Abbie froze, glancing between the two.

She hadn't even considered the implications of the fact that they were werewolves. She should have known there was going to be a social structure, and she was causing tension between an undeserving Beta and a jealous Alpha.

Simon's gaze met hers, a faint blush spreading across his face as a knowing smile played on his lips.

"Morning," He said nonchalantly.

"Morning," she murmured, the unspoken tension crackling between them.

"Hey, sleepyhead," Tamsen greeted her with a smile, despite the fact that he *clearly* hadn't been anything near happy just a moment ago. "Hope you slept well."

Abbie gave a shy nod, a slight blush creeping into her cheeks as she recalled the previous night's events.

"Y-Yeah, I did, thanks. Bed was big and comfy. Thanks for giving me the whole tent, Simon, it was really sweet of you to offer to sleep outside last night."

Sure, it might have sounded awkward and forced, but the Alpha seemed to buy it.

"We were just talking about the plan," Simon said, eager to get on a different topic. "We need to figure out how to get into the castle without getting caught."

"The only way in is through the front gate, or from the dungeons below," Tamsen explained, "but there's no way they'd let us in with their guard up. We're gonna need a distraction, for sure."

"We could strip Simon to his underwear and make him run through the castle's front lawn- I think that would be enough of a distraction," Jett suggested with a yawn, earning himself a scowl from the redhead. "If I were the Prince, he'd have all my attention, that's for sure."

"Fuck off," Simon muttered.

"Or, you could pretend to be a traveling minstrel and sing them a song," Jett quipped. "They'd probably throw you in the dungeon just to shut you up."

"I'm not singing for the vampires, Birdbrain," Simon retorted, his tone dripping with annoyance.

"Easy, boys," Tamsen said, his voice laced with frustration.

"What about the Arcane?" Abbie asked, interrupting the bickering. "We could use magic to disguise ourselves."

Jett laughed, while Tamsen seemed bewildered by the stupidity of the statement.

"Oh, and why not just say some mumbo-jumbo and levitate over the castle walls?" Jett retorted. "Arcane doesn't work on a whim, Darling."

"The Arcane has a cost," Tamsen said, paying little mind to Jett's joke. "And it's a cost I'm not willing to pay, if I can avoid it."

"There are other ways to get in, right? Maybe we could scale the walls," Abbie suggested, her brow furrowed in thought.

"If we're going to do that, we should do it at night, when the guards are less likely to notice us," Simon chimed in, trying to diffuse the tension.

"That's the first smart thing you've said all morning," Jett remarked, rolling his eyes.

"But how are we going to distract the guards so we can get past them?" Simon asked.

"Maybe we could cause a diversion somewhere else in the castle. That way, they'd have to send a bunch of their soldiers to deal with it," Abbie suggested.

"We could set a fire in the dungeons," Tamsen said, a hint of mischief glinting in his eyes. "First, we split up, and the first group tries to get in through the dungeons, the other scales the walls. Both have a distraction so we confuse them. We get rid of them and meet back up in the throne room."

"That's perfect!" Abbie exclaimed. "And we can rescue the prisoners while we're there."

"And I know exactly where we can find the necessary supplies," Jett chimed in.

"How much is it gonna cost us?" Tamsen grumbled, arching a brow.

"Not a single copper," Jett smirked. "It's on the house."

Tamsen shot him a dubious look, but he nodded nonetheless.

"Alright. So, we have a plan," Tamsen announced, his tone resolute. "Let's move out."

As they set out, Abbie fell into step beside Simon, the air buzzing with a charged energy.

"Last night," she began, her voice a hushed whisper. "I hope it wasn't...too much."

Simon blushed, glancing away.

"It wasn't," he murmured. "I liked it. I like you, Abbie."

She smiled, her gaze softening.

"I like you, too, Simon."

As they walked side by side, their hands brushed together, the gentle touch sending sparks of electricity through their fingertips.

Their eyes met, a moment of shared understanding passing between them.

They would fight side by side, a powerful force to be reckoned with.

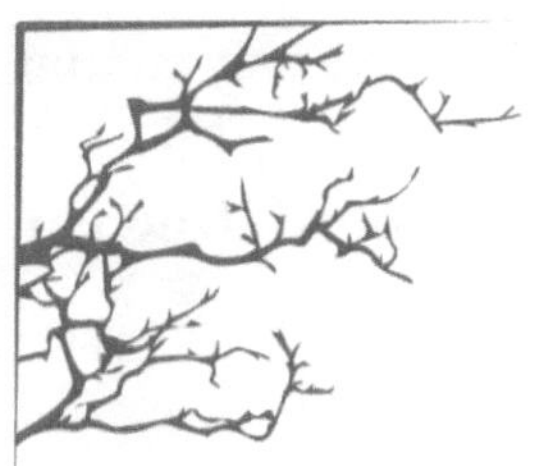

Chapter Six

Jett observed with a keen eye the blossoming connection between the two companions. Their chemistry wasn't lost on him, evident in the subtle glances, the lingering moments of shared laughter, and the unspoken tension that seemed to weave itself between them.

"Well, well, well, looks like we've got a couple of lovebirds on our hands," Jett quipped, relishing the reaction it earned from Tamsen, who shot him a scowl that could sour milk.

"Can it, Jett. I'll break your fucking jaw." Tamsen retorted sharply, his voice laced with a hint of menace that sent a shiver down the spine of anyone within earshot.

"Oh, please. You wouldn't dare. You can't deny what's right in front of your eyes, big guy."

Tamsen rolled his eyes, feigning annoyance as he picked up the pace.

"I said, can it."

"You know, you really should just ask the girl out. It's not like you have anything to lose," Jett taunted.

The low, guttural growl that emanated from Tamsen conveyed more threat than words ever could.

"I swear, Jett. If you don't shut the fuck up, I'll-"

"You'll what?" Jett teased, flashing him a wolfish grin.

Tamsen let out an exasperated sigh, running a hand through his hair.

"I'm going to strangle you, and you better not fucking enjoy it."

"Oh, *please*," Jett scoffed, seemingly unfazed. "You know I'm right. You're just afraid to admit it."

"You're not exactly the epitome of charming yourself," Tamsen shot back.

"Maybe not, but I'm honest about it.," Jett shrugged, a smirk dancing on his lips. "You're a stubborn ass who's afraid to let himself feel something."

"I don't know what the fuck you're talking about," Jett persisted, undeterred by Tamsen's attempts to silence him. "And neither do you, so do us both a favor and shut your mouth."

"Really? Because it seems pretty clear to me. You're interested in Abbie, but you're too scared to do anything about it."

"That's bullshit. I don't have any interest in her." Tamsen stated firmly, trying to dismiss the conversation.

"Whatever you say, big guy. Keep lying to yourself."

The atmosphere grew heavy with unspoken words and unresolved emotions as they trekked through the forest. The day progressed, the sun casting its warm glow through the foliage, painting the forest floor with shifting patterns of light and shade.

As the afternoon waned, a gentle breeze swept through the clearing, carrying with it the fragrant scent of wildflowers and fresh grass, providing a momentary respite from the intensity of their exchange.

"We should stop for the day," Simon announced, the first of them to succumb to the exhaustion of the rough ride. "I'm hungry..."

"We'll reach the village by nightfall," Tamsen replied, his tone terse.

"We don't want to go in too late. It'll be dark by the time we get there, and the streets will be crawling with guards." Simon argued.

"Besides," Jett added, giving a mischievous wink, "we should take the chance to rest up. Who knows what kinds of adventures we'll have once we arrive?"

Tamsen rolled his eyes, a low growl escaping his lips.

"You're an idiot."

"Aw, come on. You can't resist a challenge, and I'm just giving you one."

Tamsen sighed, pinching the bridge of his nose in exasperation. "Fine. We'll rest for the night. But if anything happens, I'm holding you *personally* responsible."

"I wouldn't expect anything less," Jett retorted, a smug grin etched upon his lips.

As the afternoon gave way to dusk, the group made camp in a secluded glade. Tamsen and Jett sparred while Simon and Abbie watched, the redhead teaching the girl a few moves.

"Here," Simon said, handing her a wooden training sword. "Try to hit me."

Abbie hesitated, her brow furrowing. "I don't know, Simon. I've never fought anyone before."

"Well, you did have a hell of a swing back there," He laughed a little, pulling down his shirt to expose his shoulder- which was adorned with a black-and-blue badge of honor. "I think I'm lucky to be alive with you on the prowl."

"I'm sorry," She muttered, looking away. "I don't want to hurt you. I was scared..."

"It's okay. Just try to land a hit," Simon urged, a faint smile tugging at the corners of his lips. "I'm not that fast, it won't be too hard. I just want to make sure you can fight Jett off if he gets too obnoxious."

"Are you sure about this, Simon?" Abbie asked, her voice wavering.

"Positive," Simon assured her.

With a determined look, Abbie raised her weapon and lunged at Simon, the impact reverberating through her bones.

Simon smiled, the excitement sparking in his eyes.

"Again," he commanded.

"I'm not sure I can, Simon," Abbie protested.

"You can do it. Just a few more times," Simon encouraged.

With a deep breath, Abbie steadied herself and lunged again, her strikes becoming more precise with each blow.

"That's it! Keep going!" Simon cheered.

"I'm not sure I can," Abbie admitted, her arms trembling from the effort.

"Just a little more. You're doing great," Simon coaxed.

Abbie took a deep breath and gathered her strength, launching a final strike.

The sword landed squarely against Simon's chest, knocking the breath from his lungs. He took a moment to recover before he smiled, pride radiating from him.

"Well done, Abbie. You're a natural."

"Really?" Abbie asked, her voice laced with disbelief.

"Absolutely," Simon assured her, placing a hand on her shoulder.

Jett scoffed, interrupting their exchange.

"That was pathetic," he taunted, a smirk plastered across his lips. "Letting a girl beat you? No way you would stand a chance against me."

"Oh, shut up, Jett," Simon retorted, his expression morphing into a scowl.

"Why don't you make me?" Jett challenged, stepping closer.

Simon glared at him, his fists clenching.

"I swear, I'll punch you in the face if you don't back off."

"Come on, Simon. I'm not scared of you," Jett sneered, a smug grin stretching his lips.

"You should be," Simon warned, his stance becoming defensive.

"Children, please," Tamsen growled as he stirred beneath a nearby tree, trying to take a nap in the afternoon shade. "Can you grow up for a minute and act like adults?"

"He started it," Simon protested, pointing an accusing finger at Jett.

"Did not," Jett scoffed.

"Did so," Simon countered, his tone indignant.

"Did not," Jett rebutted.

"Did-"

"Both of you, shut up!" Tamsen snarled, the air around him crackling with power.

Simon and Jett exchanged a sheepish glance, a faint blush coloring their cheeks.

"Now, if you'll excuse me, I'm trying to get some rest," Tamsen muttered, his eyes falling closed once more.

"I think I'm going to take a break, guys," Abbie said, but before Simon could protest, she left him alone to continue his thought-provoking argument with another *extremely intelligent individual*.

She sat next to Tamsen, both of them nestled comfortably beneath the gentle shade of the tree's canopy. Abbie giggled, bemused by their bickering banter. It was like one big- albiet occasionally grumpy- family, with each of them an equally irreplaceable link in the chain, and equally a thorn in eachother's side.

"They're cute," she commented, her voice soft.

"Who, the two idiots fighting over there?" Tamsen grumbled, cracking open an eye. "I lost track of who was winning a long time ago."

"Yeah," Abbie replied, a faint blush tinting her cheeks.

Tamsen arched a brow, a slight smirk tugging at the corner of his lips.

"They're idiots, but they're my idiots."

"I guess we all need our own idiots, huh?" Abbie smiled, a warm feeling spreading through her chest.

"Yeah," Tamsen chuckled. "I suppose we do."

"They're like brothers, aren't they?" Abbie remarked, nodding subtly toward Simon and Jett, who were now engaged in a friendly mock-wrestling match nearby.

Tamsen's gaze lingered on the pair, a hint of nostalgia flashing across his eyes before he averted his gaze.

"They are... they've been by my side through thick and thin. They're... important."

As the conversation meandered, and the night enveloped them in its quiet embrace, Abbie observed the subtle shifts in Tamsen's demeanor. His usually stoic expression softened with a tinge of vulnerability that escaped only in fleeting moments. Abbie caught the brief hesitation in his voice, an unspoken weight hidden within his words.

"Like family?" she probed gently.

Tamsen's lips quirked into a half-smile, though the pain behind it was evident. "Something like that. We all have our reasons for sticking together, I suppose. Sometimes, it's about finding a family where you least expect it."

Abbie sensed the guardedness in his tone, a veil over the deeper truths he held close. She didn't push, respecting the boundaries he had set, but her curiosity lingered like an unspoken question in the night air.

"You know, sometimes the past shapes us more than we'd like to admit," Abbie murmured, her gaze fixed on the shifting patterns in the fire. "I've seen a lot, Tamsen. Seen what it's like to have everything one moment, and the next-"

A soft sigh escaped her.

Tamsen glanced toward the horizon, a distant sadness flickering in his eyes.

"I've seen things most people couldn't imagine," Tamsen began, his voice barely above a whisper, as if testing the waters of confession. "Sometimes the things we inherit aren't just about bloodlines. They're about pain, choices, and the darkness that lingers."

"Yeah, it's a tangled mess, isn't it? We carry pieces of it with us, whether we want to or not."

"My father... he wasn't kind. Drove my mother away-" He began, before looking away. Guilt and shame flickered across his features, and for the first time since she'd met him, his resolve broke. His eyes shimmered with unshed tears, but he refused to let them fall. He couldn't. Not in front of Abigail.

"...she was a mage. I'm a result of that... a half-breed alpha, not exactly something that's celebrated."

Abbie caught a glimpse of the double life Tamsen had been living-constantly torn with the conflict between the legacy of his lineage and the scars of his upbringing. She offered a gentle smile, a silent acknowledgment of his unspoken stories.

"It's not easy, finding your place," she offered softly, keeping her gaze fixed on the dancing flames. "Sometimes, the people who are supposed to be family... aren't really family at all."

Tamsen's jaw clenched almost imperceptibly, a fleeting glimpse of pain crossing his features before he masked it with practiced ease.

"You're right about that, Abigail."

Their conversation ebbed into a comfortable silence, the unspoken understanding between them weaving a fragile bond. Abbie sensed there was more to Tamsen's story, pieces he guarded fiercely, locked away behind a facade of strength and resilience. She respected what was left unspoken, knowing that some wounds were too deep to be revealed in the flickering glow of a campfire.

"You're not alone," She said, putting her hand on his. He was warm, so warm, his heart beating a frantic rhythm. His eyes widened for a moment, surprised at the kindness of her gesture, but something made him recoil from the touch.

"I think I'm going to take a walk," He announced, an edge to his voice. "Thanks for... everything, Abbie."

Tamsen rose from his seat by the dwindling fire, an air of restlessness enveloping him. His movements were jagged, uneasy, unlike the confident Alpha she had grown to know. With a glance toward Abbie, he offered a faint smile before pacing the periphery of the camp. All of it hinted at a mind preoccupied by turbulent thoughts, something he had kept to himself for so long.

The rhythmic sound of his footsteps echoed softly against the backdrop of the night, a cadence that matched the weight of his unsettled mind. He traced a path amidst the trees, under the guise of keeping watch for the night. As Tamsen paced restlessly around the camp, Abbie sought solace in her sketchbook. The pages lay open before her, blank spaces awaiting inspiration. Her hand moved almost instinctively, the charcoal tracing lines and curves, capturing the flickering light and the silhouette of the pacing figure.

Abbie watched him quietly. She observed the subtle tension in his shoulders, the occasional clenching of his jaw- an outward manifestation of an inner turmoil he seemed unable to voice.

Unaware of her subconscious focus, Abbie's strokes melded effortlessly onto the page. The faint scratch of charcoal against paper echoed in the quietude of the night. Her gaze darted between Tamsen and the sketchbook, each glance at him translating into deliberate lines on the sheet.

Lost in the creative trance, Abbie's hand moved with an innate grace, guided by unseen muses. The sketch began to take form, capturing the essence of Tamsen's restlessness- the furrowed brow, the determined stride, the intensity etched in every line of his being. Abbie hadn't noticed how every stroke had shaped his features onto the paper, the graphite outlining the complexities of his expressions, the shadows playing on his face.

As he circled back toward the campfire, his gaze lingered on the horizon, the distant line where the sky met the land.

"You okay, Tamsen?" Abbie inquired softly, her voice cutting through the tranquil night.

Tamsen halted his pacing, his gaze fixing on the flickering flames before meeting Abbie's concerned eyes. His lips curved into a rueful smile tinged with a hint of resignation. "Just restless, Abigail. Sometimes the past catches up with you, no matter how far you run."

He turned towards Abbie, his eyes falling upon the sketchbook cradled in her hands. His steps drew him closer, curiosity mingling with a hint of surprise.

"What are you drawing?" Tamsen's voice broke the serene atmosphere.

Abbie looked up, startled, as if returning from a distant reverie. Her eyes widened slightly, realizing she had inadvertently sketched Tamsen. *All of him.* Every detail, all forever etched into the worn, leather-bound pages. A faint blush crept onto her cheeks as she hesitated, flipping the book shut almost protectively.

"Oh, it's nothing," she stammered, attempting to conceal the artwork. "Just doodling, you know?"

Tamsen's curiosity piqued, and with gentle persistence, he reached for the sketchbook. Abbie relinquished it hesitantly, her heart pounding with apprehension. Tamsen flipped through the pages until he landed on the sketch she had been working on.

The campfire's light danced upon the drawing, illuminating the intricacies of the sketch. Tamsen's eyes widened in surprise, a subtle flicker of recognition crossing his features. His gaze shifted from the sketch to Abbie, a mix of emotions playing across his face- astonishment, intrigue, and a touch of vulnerability.

"This... it's me," Tamsen murmured, his voice tinged with a hint of wonder.

Abbie glanced away, feeling exposed, yet she nodded hesitantly.

"I'm sorry, I didn't mean to... I was just lost in drawing."

Tamsen studied the sketch, his expression softening as he traced the lines with a careful fingertip. "You're incredibly talented, Abigail. You've captured something... something I hadn't realized was there."

"It might just take a little looking to see it," She replied, tucking a lock of hair behind her ear. "And someone who knows what to look for."

The air hung heavy with tension as Tamsen tentatively broached the offer, his voice lacking its usual confidence.

"Abbie, after all this is over, if you want... you can stay with us. With the pack."

Abbie's breath caught in her throat, her heart racing at the unexpected proposal.

She hadn't put a lot of thought into what comes after. What would happen if they succeeded in killing the Caeds? How would the kingdom fare without the vampires overruling it?

What would her and Iris do when they got out?

They couldn't return to the village. Part of her didn't *want* to return home, even if it was possible- a deep hatred for their father had been brewing beneath the surface, a bitterness at the thought of the old man's slimy hands signing Iris' life away.

So there wasn't any "home" to return to.

Still...

The mere idea of residing among werewolves, despite the camaraderie she had developed with them, sent a shiver down her spine. Her mind raced with conflicting emotions, torn between the safety of companionship and the fear of the unknown.

"I... I don't know, Tamsen," she stammered, her voice betraying the turmoil within. "It's just... living with werewolves, it's a lot to take in."

Tamsen, sensing her unease, retracted slightly, a flicker of hurt flashing across his features almost imperceptibly before he masked it behind the veil of a forced smile.

"Right. Sorry for suggesting it."

Before Abbie could gather her thoughts to explain further, Tamsen retreated from the campsite with an air of quiet resignation. Her heart sank at the abrupt turn of events, the weight of her words hanging heavily in the air. She had inadvertently wounded him with her hesitation, and the guilt already gnawed at her.

Driven by a surge of remorse and the need to clarify, Abbie hurried after Tamsen, her footsteps quickening as she ventured into the shadowed woods. She found him a short distance away, his form tense as he stood with his back to her, his silhouette framed against the moonlit clearing.

"Tamsen, wait," Abbie called out softly, her voice tinged with urgency.

He turned to face her, his features etched with a mix of hurt and defeat.

"You don't have to explain, Abigail. I get it."

"No, it's not like that," Abbie insisted, her words rushed and filled with regret. "I didn't mean to hurt you. It's just... it's a big decision, and I... I got overwhelmed."

Tamsen's gaze softened momentarily, but a veil of sorrow lingered in his eyes.

"But maybe it's better if I go."

"Tamsen-"

In a breathtaking display of nature's mystery, his silhouette contorted and stretched, the moonlight tracing intricate patterns across his changing figure. Bones shifted, muscles rearranged beneath his skin, as if an unseen sculptor reshaped his very essence.

The once-familiar features dissolved, melding into a majestic creature- a *wolf*, its fur a tapestry of silvery hues shimmering under the moon's tender embrace.

Abbie stood mesmerized, witnessing the beauty of the transformation- the ethereal creature before her radiated a primal grace, an embodiment of raw power and untamed wilderness. Yet within those piercing eyes, she recognized the familiarity of a friend, a connection that bridged the realms of human and supernatural.

As the magnificent wolf turned away, vanishing into the depths of the forest, Abbie remained rooted to the spot, her breath caught in the poignant dance between wonder and acceptance of the unknown.

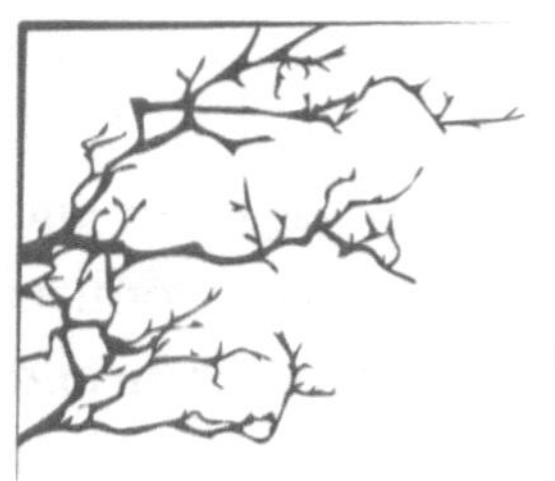

Chapter Seven

"Abbie!"

The distant call of her name shattered her reverie, the echo of Simon's voice slicing through the night's stillness. She tore her gaze away from the spot where Tamsen had vanished, a tumult of emotions raging within her as she grappled with the weight of her decision.

The forest seemed to hold its breath, enveloping her in a cloak of uncertainty as she stood suspended between the desire to follow Tamsen and the pull of responsibility to return to camp. Her heart felt torn, the longing for understanding and acceptance warring against the practicality of her situation.

"Abigail! Where are you?!"

Simon's voice rang out once more. Abbie took a deep, steadying breath, her resolve firming despite the ache in her chest. With a final glance toward the depths where Tamsen had disappeared, she turned, retracing her steps back to the campsite.

Each footfall felt like lead, the tangled emotions swirling within her like the whispering wind that wound through the trees. She wove her way through the forest, the moonlight guiding her path, yet her mind remained tethered to the haunting image of Tamsen's transformation.

As she approached the familiar glow of the campfire, Abbie felt a pang of conflict gnawing at her.

I barely spent a few days with them, and I'm already causing so much turmoil between the pack...

Simon's voice grew louder, a note of relief evident in his tone as he spotted her returning figure. "Abbie, there you are! We were worried."

Abbie stepped into the camp's circle of light, the warmth of the fire offering solace amidst the shadows that danced around her.

Without a word, Abbie closed the distance between them and wrapped her arms around Simon in a tight embrace. It was a wordless gesture, an unspoken acknowledgment of gratitude for his concern and a silent reassurance that she was back, safe within the embrace of their makeshift family.

Simon hesitated for a moment, surprised by the sudden gesture, before returning it with equal warmth. His arms enveloped her in a comforting hold, offering silent support without probing for explanations. They stood intertwined for a fleeting moment, the crackling fire serving as a backdrop to their silent communion.

"Abbie," Simon began, his voice laced with a mixture of hesitancy and earnestness, "last night, when we shared the bed... it was nice. Do you think... we could do that again tonight?"

Abbie's breath caught, her heart fluttering at the unexpected proposition. She met his gaze, noticing the genuine sincerity in his eyes, a silent plea tinged with an unspoken desire for closeness.

"Yeah, I'd like that," Abbie replied softly, her voice carrying a delicate vulnerability of its own.

She helped him finish pitching the tent for the night, while Jett had apparently spent most of the night grooming himself. He was clean shaven, his hair in dark wet wisps from his multiple baths in the stream. He seemed rather enthralled between the shininess of the blades he had laid out on the grass and his own reflection within. The others didn't seem phased by the change, in fact, there even seemed to be a hint of relief at the fact that he was preoccupied rather than harassing someone+.

"Is he always like that?" Abbie whispered to Simon as the tent was finally ready.

"He's...different than us," Simon offered. "Shifter, yes, but not a werewolf, per se."

"What?!" Abbie began, but then Simon pressed a finger to her lips.

"Let him be. It's not often that he's not being a pain in the ass."

"O-okay..." Abbie hesitated, glancing at Jett one last time before she crawled into the tent.

Simon rolled out the soft wool bedroll, and Abbie got inside.

"It's a little warm tonight," Simon said, a hint of a blush along his cheeks as he picked at the hem of his shirt. "Is it okay if I take this off?"

"Your tent, your rules," Abbie replied with a smile.

He nodded, slowly stripping off each piece of clothing. Abbie though he'd stop at just the shirt, but no- off came his socks, pants, and trousers.

Abbie's mouth almost watered at the sight of him- primal muscles lining his entire body, his pale skin glistening with sweat. She looked away before wiggling beneath the covers, hoping he wouldn't notice her gawking at him.

"You *sure* this is okay?" He asked hesitantly as he eased himself in next to her.

The warmth of his touch, the reassuring closeness, ignited a cascade of emotions within Abbie- a blend of longing, uncertainty, and a burgeoning connection that felt both exhilarating and unfamiliar. She nestled closer to him, feeling the rhythmic rise and fall of his breath, a silent reassurance in the shared vulnerability of the moment.

"Y-yeah," Abbie stammered, her body melting into his warmth.

Their bodies aligned in a natural harmony, the unspoken tension between unexplored. Words hung in the air, suspended in the delicate balance of silent desires and uncharted territories, each heartbeat echoing the question of what lay ahead.

"Simon," She began, poking her head out from beneath the blanket, choosing her words carefully. "I think...I think I might stay with the pack after we get Iris out."

"Really?" He said, his breath catching in his throat. "That's- that's amazing!"

"It's just... there's something intriguing about them. The bond, the connection- it feels different, you know?"

Simon's heart skipped a beat, the realization that Abbie might become a permanent part of their pack sending a rush of emotions through him. He shifted closer, their breaths mingling in the hushed night air, tension thickening the space between them.

"Yeah, they're... they're good people," Simon murmured, his voice barely above a whisper. His hand moved tentatively to brush a stray strand of Abbie's hair away from her face, his touch carrying a warmth that sent tingles down her spine.

In the charged silence that followed, an electric anticipation filled the air.

Their gazes locked.

Time seemed to slow.

Simon leaned in closer, the distance between their lips almost nonexistent.

As he hovered inches away from Abbie, a sudden surge of nerves gripped Simon. His breath hitched, uncertainty flashing across his eyes at the precipice of this intimate moment. The weight of the unspoken, the fear of misjudgment, held him captive in that fleeting instant.

He hesitated, the momentum hanging suspended between them, before pulling back slightly, his gaze dropping in a mix of nervousness and regret.

"Abbie, I... I don't want to rush things. I don't want to make things complicated."

Abbie's heart skipped a beat, a whirlwind of emotions swirling within her- disappointment mingled with understanding. She managed a soft smile, masking the tug of her own feelings.

"I get it, Simon. We have time."

In the warmth of their closeness, Abbie shifted slightly, snuggling comfortably against Simon's side, their bodies fitting together in a natural rhythm. His arm draped protectively around her, offering a sense of security amidst the uncertainty that lingered in their hearts.

With each passing moment, the tension between them dissipated, replaced by a soothing calmness that enveloped them like a soft blanket. They lay intertwined, the rise and fall of their chests synchronizing in a silent symphony of shared comfort.

Underneath the canopy of stars that adorned the night sky, their whispered conversations tapered off into a contented silence. The tranquil stillness of the night cradled them in its gentle embrace, a sanctuary where worries ebbed away.

SHE DREAMT OF HIM AGAIN.

Abigail's hands were bound above her head, fastened firmly to the oak. The bark was rough against her back, but the dappled sunlight above casted a gentle warmth on her skin. The soft moans beneath the cloth gag were drowned out by the hum of insects and the rustle of trees. She could feel something around her neck- something snug, but not uncomfortable.

It felt like leather.

A collar, maybe?

The thought made her shiver with anticipation.

She squirmed as his warm fingers danced over her thighs, tracing delicate patterns over her skin. His voice whispered in her ear, words that were not words, yet still held meaning. He promised her everything she wanted, and more, if she would only surrender. She longed to give in, but something held her back, a nagging fear that she could not escape.

A shadow passed before the sun, blotting out the light.

His breath was hot on her neck as he teased her, his hands never ceasing their movements. The bindings dug into her wrists as she writhed in pleasure, his fingers working their magic.

She was his now.

And she knew it.

Still, the nagging doubt lingered.

A cold breeze swept through the glade.

He kissed her with such force that it took her breath away. She could feel the strength of his passion, his desire for her. He had claimed her as his own, and she belonged to him now. The shadows grew longer, the forest darkening around them.

Something moved in the trees.

She gave herself to him, losing herself in his embrace. He was all that mattered now, all that she needed. He filled her with such ecstasy that she thought she might die from it.

"Simon..." She moaned, arching her back.

"Shh..."

Something was watching them.

He pulled the gag from her mouth, his lips pressing against hers, his tongue plunging in to explore, intertwining with hers. He tasted like honey, and she drank deeply of his sweetness. The shadows seemed to press in on them, but she was too lost in his kiss to care.

"Simon..."

A low growl sounded from the edge of the glade, and a pair of crimson eyes peered at them from the undergrowth. Abigail froze, her heart racing. Simon didn't seem to notice, his hands roaming over her body, his kisses growing more insistent.

"Simon...we need to stop."

The eyes drew nearer, a black shape emerging from the darkness.

"What is it, my love?" He asked, nuzzling her neck.

"I think we're being watched..."

The growl grew louder, the shadows darker.

Simon laughed, kissing her again.

"Don't worry, my sweet. It's just the wind."

But the growls didn't stop.

They only grew louder.

Abigail pulled away, her eyes wide with fear. The creature stepped into the light, its fur bristling, its teeth bared. It was huge, easily twice the size of Simon.

"It's not the wind," she whispered. "We need to go, now!"

But Simon didn't seem to hear her. He was too lost in her, his kisses becoming more and more heated. Abigail tugged at the ropes, trying to free herself, but they were too tight.

"Simon, please!"

"Mmm...you taste so good," he murmured, his hands roaming over her body. The creature stalked towards them, its growl echoing through the glade. Abigail whimpered, tears stinging her eyes.

"Please, Simon! You have to listen to me!"

"I don't have to do anything," he said, his voice a low rumble. "But you have to just relax and enjoy this..."

Abigail moaned desperately into the gag, her eyes fluttering open-

THE SOFT MORNING LIGHT filtered through the seams of the tent, and the cool breeze of dawn kissed her skin. Her heart pounded in her chest, and her body trembled with the aftershocks of her dream. Simon was still there, holding her close against his his chest.

Her face turned a shade of deep crimson when it settled in that this was the second time she'd slept with him, the second time he hadn't tried to make a move, and the second time she'd dreamt about fucking him. Even if this one hadn't ended as peaceful as the last, it still made her feel guilty.

"Damn it," She whispered, trying to untangle herself from him.

He let out a whimper when she slipped away, but he didn't wake. A few stirs of discomfort later, soft snores filled the tent, and Abbie took the opportunity to slip out into the night air.

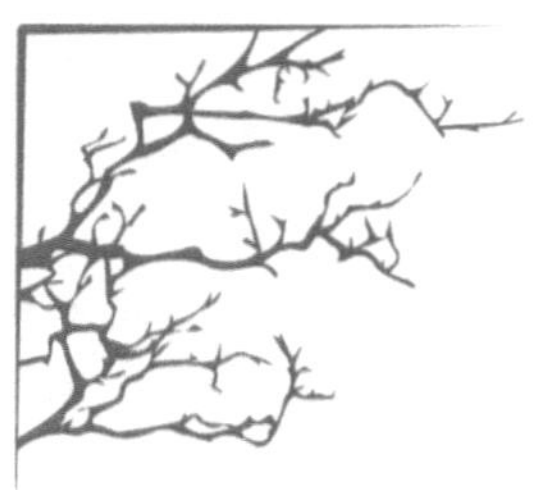

Chapter Eight

When morning came, the sun rose and shone down upon the group, illuminating the dew-covered leaves and flowers of the forest. Simon's eyes fluttered open, the bright rays of sunlight piercing the canvas tent and warming his skin. He yawned, stretching his limbs before slipping from the bedroll and dressing himself.

He stepped outside, taking a deep breath and relishing the crisp, fresh air. Abbie had been the first awake, but the others still remained in their tents.

A small stream trickled nearby, the sound of the water against the rocks almost drowned out by the morning birdsong. Insects had just started to come to life, filling the air with their droning hum.

The sketchbook laid open in Abbie's lap, charcoal etchings lining the worn parchment paper, bound by a flimsy leather string. Despite its crude appearance, it was clearly a well-loved book, the pages crinkled and dog-eared from frequent use.

"What are you drawing?" Simon asked, his curiosity getting the better of him.

Abbie blushed, a sheepish look crossing her face.

"Nothing," she muttered, hurriedly closing the sketchbook.

"Don't stop on my account," he protested, a hint of disappointment lingering in his tone.

Abbie hesitated, biting her lower lip as she debated how much to reveal. Finally, she relented, opening the sketchbook once more and gesturing to the page.

"It's not done yet," she mumbled, her cheeks flaming with embarrassment.

Simon peered down at the image, a stunned look crossing his features. It was a portrait of him, sketched in delicate lines of charcoal, every detail carefully rendered.

She didn't want to mention that she had already drawn Tamsen, and it felt odd to not have a piece of the rest of the crew embedded into the pages.

"This is...this is amazing, Abbie," he breathed, his voice laced with awe.

Abbie ducked her head, a shy smile gracing her lips.

"Maybe...stay a little? I could use a model, and it doesn't seem like the others are up yet. I don't want to rush the plan, so some time here won't hurt anything, right?" Abbie asked.

Simon nodded, a faint blush tinting his cheeks.

"Yeah, of course," he murmured, settling down next to her.

As the morning light filtered through the trees, Simon found himself transfixed by Abbie's beauty. He couldn't tear his eyes away, drinking in every detail of her face. Her long blonde hair fell in soft waves down her shoulders, and her eyes shone with a radiant glow.

"You're beautiful," he breathed, his voice barely audible.

Abbie blushed, ducking her head in embarrassment.

"No, really," Simon insisted, gently cupping her chin and tilting her head back up.

"You're not so bad yourself," Abbie murmured, her voice barely above a whisper.

Their breaths swirled in the morning chill, a closeness between them that she wanted so badly to close. She wanted to kiss him, to ease him into being confident to do all those things she'd been dreaming about.

But alas, fate wouldn't have it that way.

"Hey, where'd you run off?!" Tamsen's voice called from the camp, shattering the morning stillness.

"Over here!" Simon replied, his tone casual as he stepped back. Abbie closed her sketchbook with a soft thud, tucking it into her bag.

"Ah, there you are," Tamsen grinned, approaching them.

"You're up early," Abbie commented, giving a small wave.

"Couldn't sleep," Tamsen shrugged, settling down beside them. "I let my wolf go for a run last night, and I'm still pretty wound up."

"You okay?" Simon asked, trying not to make him aware of what had almost happened between him and Abbie.

"I'm fine. Just a lot on my mind," Tamsen replied, flashing a reassuring smile.

"If you're sure..." Simon murmured, unconvinced.

"I'm sure," Tamsen reassured him. "We've got a big day ahead of us, and I need to stay focused."

"So, what's the plan for today?" Abbie asked, trying to lighten the mood.

"We're heading into the city," Tamsen said. "There's no avoiding it, and we can't waste any more time. First, I need to see what Abbie's experience is in the Arcane. If she can use magic, she's more use to us than you lot."

"Hey," Simon protested.

"You guys are good fighters, but we need all the help we can get."

"Fair enough," Simon sighed. "Fine, I'll start packing, and I'll leave you to it."

With a last hesitant glance, Simon stood, returning to the tents.

"So, what can you do?" Tamsen asked, turning to Abbie.

"Not much," she admitted.

"Do you understand the art of Sapping?" The air was filled with a gentle breeze that carried the fragrance of blossoms. His weathered hands, roughened by years of experience, delicately plucked a small dandelion, its vibrant yellow petals seemingly aglow under the sun's tender caress. With a subtle turn, he redirected his attention to Abbie, his eyes holding a depth of knowledge and ancient wisdom.

"Arcane magic requires a source. A fuel. And it isn't always pretty."

Tamsen's fingertips traced the delicate contours of the dandelion's petals. A spectral shift occurred; hues dulled, vitality seeped away, and life relinquished its hold. The once vibrant bloom crumbled, dissolving into a whisper of dust.

"Incredible," she said, barely above a whisper.

"This is the essence of Arcane," Tamsen explained solemnly. "The art of harnessing energy, though seldom practiced due to its dire implications. Only the most desperate are driven to wield its power."

"That's amazing," Abbie breathed.

"It's a powerful tool. But it's also dangerous. The more power you draw, the more it can corrupt you. The more you take, the stronger the effect. You can't control it. But a rune can. Each one has a meaning, a purpose, and channeling Sapped energy into the scripture is the only way to do it safely. Even then, it's a losing game. Unless you have a teacher."

Abbie nodded, a determined look crossing her features.

"But I can learn," she vowed. "Is it safe for me to practice?"

"Not in the slightest. But girls like danger nowadays, don't they?"

He smiled, plucking another sunset-colored flower from the ground. He studied it for a moment, and then, he held it out to her.

"Can you sap the life from this?"

"How?"

"Take the stem and hold it tight, and concentrate on it. Feel the life flowing from the plant. And then, you pull it towards you."

"But...why? Won't it die?"

"Yes," Tamsen replied, his tone solemn.

After a moment of hesitation, Abbie nodded, her brow furrowed. She held the tiny flower in her palm, and she focused on the life force flowing through its stem.

"Concentrate," Tamsen murmured, his gaze fixed upon her.

She did as he commanded, her focus narrowing in on the plant. The seed began to wither, its color fading from yellow to grey. As the last remnants of life faded, a spark of power flickered within Abbie, her hand beginning to glow a faint red.

Tamsen smiled, pride radiating from him. "Well done, Abbie. You've tapped into the Arcane."

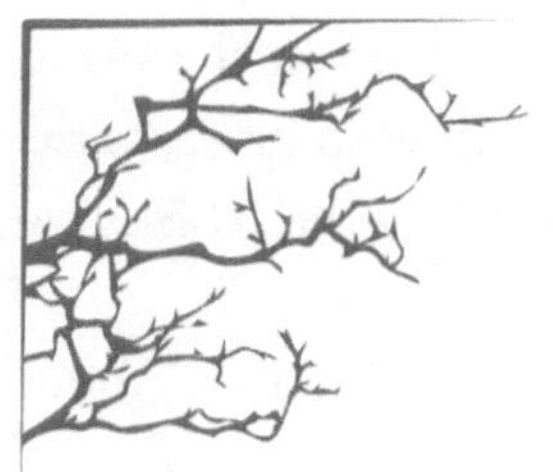

Chapter Nine

"This power," he cautioned, the lines etched on his face deepening as he spoke, "it's not a trifle. It's a gift, yes, but one that can easily turn into a curse. Handle it with utmost care."

"I understand," She replied with a nod.

"Good," Tamsen murmured, his eyes softening as he regarded her. "Now, for practice. Focus on the grass around you. Channel your newfound abilities but refrain from touching the roots. I'll teach you how to safely harness the energy later."

With each intentional thought, the grass yielded to her power. Blades once lush and verdant now curled and crisped, taking on a sepia hue as the vitality was drawn into Abbie. Waves of raw energy coursed through her, an exhilarating sensation that surpassed any she had experienced before.

As Abbie's newfound control over the Arcane brought a flicker of pride to her eyes, Tamsen's attention shifted momentarily. He scanned the surroundings, his gaze lingering on Jett, who prowled the camp with an air of restlessness, restlessly securing the bags for the trip.

Tamsen's eyes narrowed imperceptibly, a subtle flicker of concern crossing his features. He leaned in closer to Abbie, lowering his voice to a hushed tone. "Keep an eye on Jett. His raven isn't quite... cooperative lately."

"What?"

"Nevermind," Tamsen's lips curved into a forced smile, masking the depth of his worry. "He's just... dealing with something. He'll be fine."

But as Jett continued his restless pacing, the piercing gaze of his dark eyes darting between the trees, a sense of disquiet settled within the camp, a silent tension simmering beneath the facade of calm.

"Everything alright?" Simon piped up as he pulled the drawstring of his bag tight, finishing his packing.

Tamsen nodded curtly, his eyes still fixated on Jett. "Yeah, just... keeping watch. We need to stay alert. Looks like he's having quite the trouble calming the beast."

Simon followed Tamsen's gaze, his brow furrowing at the sight of Jett's agitated state.

"Should we... do something?"

Tamsen hesitated, torn between revealing Jett's inner turmoil and maintaining a semblance of normalcy. "He... he needs space. He'll sort it out."

Abbie observed Jett's troubled demeanor from afar, a sense of worry knotting in her stomach. She yearned to offer help but sensed the unspoken boundaries that surrounded Jett's inner turmoil.

His tousled, midnight-black hair cascaded in wild waves, unkempt and unruly, framing a face marked by a rugged handsomeness. He obsessively rearranged his hair, occasionally breaking his habit by looking at his reflection in the glistening steel blade he twirled in his trembling hands.

Jett's restlessness seemed to escalate, his movements becoming more erratic, a silent struggle waging within him as he battled to maintain control. Keeping his spirit-side at bay for so long, he finally began to crack at the seams, threatening to unravel the delicate balance he sought to uphold.

As he paced, a primal instinct clawed at the edges of his consciousness- a yearning, a desperation that gnawed at his resolve. He glanced furtively at Abbie, her focused determination a stark contrast to the chaos festering within him. Her newfound abilities- *and closeness to everyone in the group but him-* the emotions they stirred only fueled to losen the grip he held on himself.

"Hey, Jett," Simon's voice cut through the morning stillness, leaving an echo across the clearing. "You okay?"

A momentary lapse in his facade allowed a glimpse of vulnerability to surface- a flicker of pain, a hint of anguish that clouded his eyes before he swiftly masked it behind a mask of indifference.

"Fine. Just restless. It's nothing."

Simon studied him for a moment, a hint of concern etched on his features. "If you need anything..."

"I'm *good*," Jett dismissed with a forced nonchalance, his gaze flickering back toward Abbie, who was earnestly practicing her newly discovered abilities. "Fine, in fact- *just fine*. More than fine. Why wouldn't I be?"

"You need to go cool off, I think," Simon began, but Jett laughed half-heartedly and shook his head. "How long had it been since you shifted? A week? Longer? You need to-"

"No can do," He twirled a blade in his hands- one of his favorites- a Mercygiver, a marvel of ancient craftsmanship. It gleamed under the ambient light, its hilt adorned with delicate runes etched into shimmering silver. Yet, beneath its alluring exterior lay an otherworldly power, an arcane enchantment known only to a select few.

"Jett, please," Simon argued. "Maybe we should rest for another day."

He exhaled sharply, a heavy sigh escaping his lips as his fingers worked the knife with a precision born from a years of skill. Jett's fingers danced with a nervous energy, the knife twirling effortlessly through the air.

"No. We're leaving. We'll be fine, now that there's a mage with us, right?" He nodded towards Abbie.

Tamsen joined them, his attention focused on Abbie.

"She's a quick learner. Strong potential."

Jett nodded absently, his eyes inadvertently drawn to Abbie's radiant smile as she made progress with the Arcane. His spirit-side fluttered with agitation, a silent anxiety that threatened to unravel his carefully crafted facade.

How long had it been since someone made him feel like that?

With a practiced ease, Jett masked his inner turmoil behind a veneer of aloofness, keeping his restless raven's unrest hidden from prying eyes. The morning wore on, the camp bustling with activity, yet Jett's internal conflict simmered beneath the surface, an untamed storm that threatened to disrupt the fragile calm of their journey ahead.

Simon, Tamsen, and Abbie packed their belongings and prepared for the long trek to the next city- one last stop before the castle. Jett, on the other hand, spent the majority of the day honing his combat skills, sparring against a makeshift wooden target.

"We should get going," Simon's voice broke through the intensity of Jett's focus.

"In a moment," Jett grunted, his tone clipped.

Simon's concern was evident, furrowing his brow in worry.

"What's wrong?"

"Just a headache," Jett shook his head, the lie sticking in his throat. "Yeah, it's nothing. I'll be fine."

"We should get going," Simon repeated, not willing to push the issue.

"Okay," Jett muttered, wiping the sweat from his brow. "You guys go ahead, I'll be ready in a second."

He focused on packing the blades, his hands working mechanically, the metallic glint of the weapons offering a temporary distraction. He meticulously arranged the enchanted blades into their sheaths, each one pulsating with arcane runes that shimmered in the daylight.

Abbie approached quietly, her gaze thoughtful as she observed him arranging the weapons.

"Mind if I give you a hand?" Abbie asked, her voice gentle, yet assertive.

Jett hesitated, his fervent instincts clamoring for his attention, but Abbie's determination softened his resistance. He nodded reluctantly, though he was unable to refuse her offer.

"Sure," he mumbled, forcing a semblance of composure as he handed her a few of the blades to pack.

Abbie worked alongside him, her nimble fingers deftly sliding each weapon into its sheath, her touch sending a tingle of energy through the enchanted runes. Despite the chaotic storm raging within him, Jett found a strange sense of calm in Abbie's presence- a fleeting reprieve from what had been tormenting him.

As they packed the blades, Abbie marveled at the intricate runes adorning each weapon, her fascination evident in her bright eyes. "These runes are incredible. They hold so much power."

Jett nodded in agreement, grateful for the distraction that Abbie's curiosity provided.

"They're enchanted with protective and offensive spells. They enhance the wielder's abilities."

She examined one of the blades closely, tracing the ancient symbols etched into the metal with a sense of wonder.

"This one... it's different. The runes seem more intricate."

"It is," He said, his thoughts clouded as the fading sun caught her hair just right. "...it's special. Really special."

Suddenly, impulsively, Jett's hand brushed against Abbie's, their fingers entwining for a fleeting moment. His gaze met hers, a whirlwind of emotions dancing in the depths of his eyes- a silent plea, a hidden confession.

In that charged moment, as if guided by an unspoken force, Jett leaned in, his lips meeting Abbie's in a sudden, desperate kiss. It was a collision of silent desires, a storm of conflicting emotions, a brief surrender to the overwhelming pull of fate and instincts.

Abbie froze for a heartbeat, surprised by the suddenness of the gesture. Her mind raced, emotions tangled, yet a trace of something indefinable tugged at her heart.

Then, when she pulled back, he finally realized what he had done.

Recoiling from the impulsive act, Jett felt the weight of his actions immediately. His gaze dropped, his breaths shallow, overcome by a wave of regret and guilt. The suddenness of the kiss lingered like an echo in the quiet space around them, leaving an unspoken question hanging in the air- a question neither of them dared to voice.

Abbie stood there, speechless. Her mind raced, grappling with the sudden turn of events and the unspoken turmoil that seemed to envelop Jett.

The silence stretched, a taut thread connecting them in a fragile moment suspended in time. Neither dared to break it, both grappling with the consequences of an impulsive act that had unexpectedly shifted the dynamics between them.

Jett's throat felt dry as he finally summoned the courage to speak, his voice laden with a mix of remorse and vulnerability.

"Abbie, I- I'm sorry. That wasn't-"

"Jett, what's taking so-" Simon stood, not far from camp, his mouth hung open at the sight of the flustered pair. "What the hell is going on here?"

Jett, startled by Simon's sudden arrival, took a step back, a flicker of shame clouding his features.

"Nothing, it's not-"

"Are you kidding me?" Simon exclaimed, his eyes widening. "Did you just kiss her?"

"No, I didn't!" Jett snapped, his cheeks flushing with heat.

"Like hell you didn't! You're lying through your teeth right now," Simon accused, his voice laced with indignation. A deep growl swelled from his chest, and he took a step forward as his fists clenched. "I can fucking smell that you're a liar!"

"Simon, please-" Abbie tried to interject, but the argument had already spiraled out of control.

"I can't believe this! After all the shit we've been through, you'd do something like this? I thought you were my friend, Jett-"

"Simon, just drop it, okay? It was nothing," Jett protested, but the damage had already been done.

Simon stormed off, his rage simmering beneath the surface.

"Simon, wait-" Abbie called after him, but to no avail.

"He's right. It was a mistake," Jett muttered, the shame evident in his voice. "Let's just...get into town. I'll leave you all alone."

The tension was palpable, the silence deafening as the trio made their way to the village. Simon stewed in his anger, refusing to make eye contact with Jett, while Abbie and Tamsen exchanged worried glances, neither knowing how to diffuse the situation. Tamsen was out of the loop completely- something that Abbie was more than thankful for.

She found herself falling behind the others, her mind still occupied with the events of the day. She could feel the Arcane buzzing beneath her skin, the raw power humming through her veins.

It was exhilarating, yet terrifying.

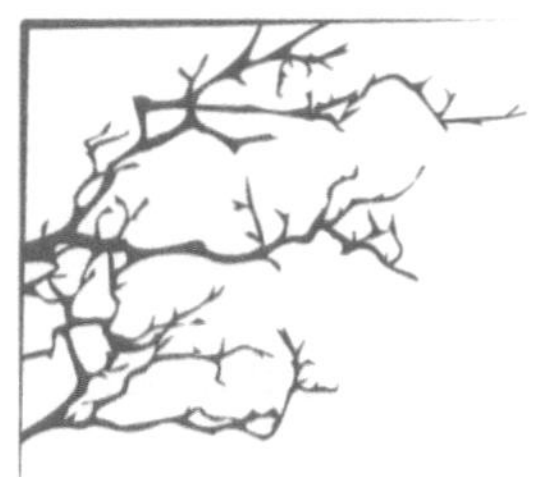

Chapter Ten

The journey to the city was filled with an uncomfortable silence, a strained tension that hovered over them like a dark cloud. Jett's inner conflict continued to wreak havoc on his emotions, while Simon's anger and hurt simmered beneath the surface, threatening to boil over at any moment.

Abbie could feel the mounting tension, her anxiety rising with each passing mile. She desperately wanted to intervene, to try and mend the rift that had opened between her friends, but she knew that Simon's anger was justified.

Finally, after what seemed like an eternity, they arrived at the edge of the village. As the buildings came into view, the group felt a collective sigh of relief, eager to escape the brewing friction between them.

As they entered the bustling town, a myriad of smells and sights greeted them. Merchants peddled their wares, the aromas of roasted meat and fresh baked bread permeating the air. Children ran and played, their laughter filling the streets. The atmosphere was vibrant and alive, a stark contrast to the strained silence that had hung over them moments earlier.

Jett's tension lessened, the sight of the village distracting him momentarily. His eyes wandered, catching the sight of Abbie's golden hair. He felt a tug in his chest, the memories of the kiss playing in his head, reliving the guilty pleasure.

He wanted her.

But the others wouldn't allow that, would they?

Abbie's attention was drawn to the various stalls and vendors, the smells and sights of the village captivating her.

"It's so beautiful here," she breathed, a smile tugging at her lips.

"Indeed, it is," Tamsen agreed, a fond look crossing his features. "When I was really little, my mom would take me to the market here. I loved the homemade sweets..."

"It seems peaceful," Abbie added. "If it wasn't so close to the castle, I wouldn't mind settling in a place like this..."

"Sometimes, even a mage and a wolf can catch a drink at the tavern there," He said, a slight smile crossing his lips. "Why don't we all meet back there tonight? Jett can get us some coin, and I'll see if I can find any other wolves that want to join in on the siege. We could use every hand we can get."

"I think that's a great idea. It will give us a chance to rest up and re-group," Abbie replied.

Tamsen nodded, his gaze flitting to Jett for a moment. "I'll see you later tonight, then. Try to keep out of trouble."

Abbie and Tamsen went their separate ways, while Simon and Jett remained in the town square.

"So, I guess this is where we part ways," Simon stated, his tone tense. "I'm just going to the tavern. I'd probably be more useful there right now."

"Simon, listen, about what happened-" Jett began, but he was sharply cut off by Simon.

"I don't want to hear it, Jett. I trusted you, and you betrayed that trust. I don't know what's gotten into you, but I need some space."

"Look, I'm *sorry*. I shouldn't have-"

"Stop, Jett. Just stop. I don't want to hear your excuses. What's done is done. We can talk about it later. I just need some time to cool off."

"Alright. I'll guess I'll see you at the tavern later?"

"Fine. I'll see you then."

With that, Simon walked off, leaving Jett alone in the center of the town square.

Jett's jaw clenched as he watched Simon's retreating figure. He was overcome with a mixture of anger and guilt, his raven flaring with frustration. He could feel the conflict brewing within him, the desire to fight and fly at war with the need to control his impulses.

"Dammit," he muttered, his fist colliding with the stone wall, a surge of pain radiating through his knuckles.

A wave of nausea and dizziness washed over him, the effects of his raven's turmoil and his injury taking its toll.

As the world began to spin, he stumbled toward a nearby tree, grasping onto it for support. His breath came in ragged gasps, his vision blurring at the edges. He struggled to maintain his composure, the conflict within him threatening to unravel his fragile facade.

He closed his eyes, a wave of nausea hitting him again. His raven fluttered agitatedly, the primal instinct fighting to gain control.

"Come on," he hissed through gritted teeth, struggling to contain the storm within. "Don't let it win. You're stronger than this. *Control it.*"

With every ounce of willpower he possessed, Jett fought against the chaos within. The struggle waged within, his raven clawing at the edges of his consciousness.

"Don't lose control," he whispered, a desperate plea to the universe. "Not here. Not now."

A few moments later, a strange calm descended over him. His breathing slowed, his heartbeat returning to normal. The internal battle ceased, his raven temporarily quelled.

As he regained his composure, his thoughts turned to the future. He could feel the uncertainty, the fear of losing himself.

He needed a way to cope, a distraction from the chaos and the torment.

"Just get rid of a few blades, get some money, easy peasy," He tried to tell himself, hoping a task to focus on would keep him temporarily occupied.

The prospect of selling his beloved weapons weighed heavily on his heart, but the alternative was unthinkable. He would do anything, sell anything, to keep his raven's turmoil at bay. He couldn't shift, because if Abbie happened to see, she would be horrified. She would have to be. She was a human.

He took a deep breath, steeling himself for the task ahead. He could do this. He had to do this. For his sanity, for his soul.

"You can do this. Just focus, and you'll be fine."

With his resolve firmly set, he straightened, his eyes scanning the crowd for potential buyers.

Amidst the lively bustle of townsfolk going about their day, Jett spotted a shadowy figure lingering near the corner of a nearby alley. The person's demeanor exuded an air of secrecy and discretion- an aura that hinted at dealings outside the law, which, in this case, suited Jett's needs perfectly.

With cautious steps, Jett approached the figure, his senses on high alert. The alley's shadows danced around the mysterious character, concealing their identity until Jett drew closer.

The figure stood cloaked in a dark mantle, their silhouette a mere shadow amid the alley's dimness. Their attire, a peculiar amalgamation of stolen mage armor, both intrigued and surprised Jett. The stolen garb, ornate and layered with ancient runes, appeared incongruent in the hands of someone who seemed more at home in the shadows than wielding the potent artifacts they donned.

Underneath the stolen armor, the figure's posture exuded a sense of coiled tension, a readiness to act at a moment's notice. A cowl partially obscured their features, leaving only a sliver of face visible beneath the hood.

The figure turned to face him, his voice a bitter hiss.

"What do you want?"

Jett hesitated for a moment, his mind racing through the careful words he needed to choose. "I've got something you might be interested in."

The figure's eyes glinted in the dim light, an unspoken curiosity emanating from behind the shadowy veil.

"Show me."

Jett carefully reached into his pack, retrieving one of the enchanted blades- a testament to ancient craftsmanship and forbidden power. As he presented the weapon, the runes shimmered faintly, hinting at the potent magic infused within its steel.

The figure's interest piqued as they examined the blade, their gloved hand running along the engraved runes. "Impressive. But what makes you think I'm interested?"

"I've got more," Jett replied, his voice deliberate and low. "And these aren't your usual fare."

The figure studied him for a moment, assessing the gravity of Jett's words.

"Where'd you get these?"

Jett's jaw tightened, a subtle tension rippling through him.

"Let's just say they're from a unique source. Authentic. Powerful."

A moment of silence passed between them, laden with unspoken implications and the weight of secrecy. The figure seemed to deliberate, contemplating the offer on the table.

"How many?" He finally asked, his voice a low whisper edged with cautious interest.

Jett considered his options, carefully weighing his next move.

"A few. But quality over quantity, right?"

The figure nodded slowly, their eyes gleaming with a calculating glint.

"Meet me tonight. Same alley. Midnight."

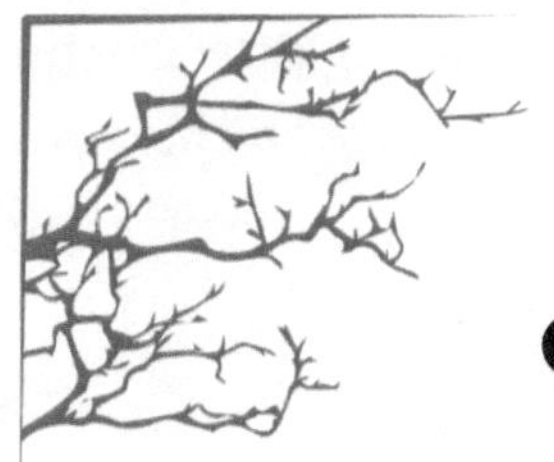

Chapter Twelve

Within the cozy ambiance of the tavern, soft amber hues casted a gentle glow across the worn wooden tables from flickering candlelight. Simon sat in a secluded corner, nursing a mug of ale with an air of palpable hurt and simmering anger. His features contorted with the raw emotions of betrayal and frustration, his eyes fixated on the swirling depths of the ale as if seeking solace within.

Abbie approached with a hesitance that matched the heavy weight in her heart. She treaded softly, cautiously inching closer to Simon, aware of the deep wounds that had unwittingly been inflicted. She settled into the seat opposite him, a sense of remorse etched in every line of her face.

"Simon," Abbie spoke gently, her voice carrying the weight of her regret. "Can we talk?"

Simon's gaze briefly flickered toward her, a tumultuous mix of pain and betrayal evident in his eyes before he turned away, his attention focused on the ale, his voice tinged with bitterness when he finally spoke.

"What's left to talk about, Abbie?"

"I'm so sorry," Abbie began, her voice laced with regret. "I know you saw... what happened."

Simon's jaw clenched, the memory of witnessing Abbie and Jett's unexpected kiss flashing vividly in his mind.

"Yeah, I saw," he muttered, a note of hurt underlying his words.

"It wasn't what you think," Abbie pleaded. "It was a mistake, a moment of confusion. I never meant to-"

"A *mistake*?" Simon interrupted, a tinge of disbelief coloring his tone. "Confusion? Is that what you call it? Enlighten me, Abbie, because I had no idea this is how humans worked."

"Please-"

"Our kind is born to seek out our fated mates," He began. "When Tamsen found me, I thought that the pack was all I'd ever know. Then I met you. Something felt different, and I just...I thought you might've been my answer."

Abbie's heart sank at the hurt etched across Simon's face, the raw vulnerability that she had inadvertently caused. She reached out, hesitantly placing a hand on his, hoping for a connection, a chance to bridge the gap that had formed between them.

"I don't know what to say, Simon," Abbie admitted, her voice tinged with sorrow. "I care about you, and I never wanted to hurt you."

Simon withdrew his hand, a pained expression crossing his face.

"You cared about me enough to... to do that?" Simon sighed heavily, his gaze fixed on the swirling contents of his mug. "I trusted you, Abbie. And him."

The silence between them grew heavy with unspoken regrets and the fracture of trust that had once bound them. Abbie struggled for words, grappling with the enormity of the mistake that had torn them apart.

Amidst the muted clatter of glasses and hushed conversations that permeated the tavern, Abbie called the bartender over, ordering a drink in a quiet, almost resigned tone. With a sigh, she placed her sketchbook on the table, her fingers grazing the parchment.

As she flipped through the pages, her gaze lingered on the sketch of Simon- a work in progress that captured his essence with intricate lines and careful strokes. With a moment's hesitation, she tore the page from the sketchbook, the torn edges a testament to the abrupt fracture between them.

Abbie approached Simon and gently placed the drawing in front of him, her eyes cast downward, unable to meet his gaze. "I started this for you. It's not finished, but... I thought you might want it."

Simon's gaze softened as he looked at the sketch, the pain in his eyes momentarily replaced by a flicker of appreciation. He traced the lines with a heavy heart, a silent acknowledgment of the connection they once shared.

As Abbie stood to leave, her voice was tinged with an unspoken sorrow.

"I'll find a way into the castle on my own. I don't want to come between you and your friends. Take care, Simon."

She turned away, her steps heavy with the weight of regrets, leaving behind a silent echo of fractured bonds and a wistful longing for what had been lost.

"Wait."

Then, in an abrupt surge of emotion, Simon rose from his seat, his hand darting out to grasp Abbie's arm firmly before she could take another step away. His eyes pleaded with a mixture of vulnerability and determination as he halted her departure.

"Abbie, please," Simon implored, his voice tinged with urgency. "Stay."

Abbie turned back, startled by the suddenness of his movement, her eyes wide with surprise and a glimmer of hope. She met his gaze, searching his eyes for the unspoken words that lay beneath his plea.

"I've never been good at standing up for myself," Simon confessed, his voice wavering with a rare vulnerability. "But... I want to stand up for you. I need to. You can't just go by yourself. I won't let you."

His grip on her arm was gentle, yet there was a steadfast resolve in his touch. His heart spilled out with words he'd long kept hidden, his desire to protect Abbie overriding his usual restraint.

"You shouldn't have to face this alone," Simon continued. "I want to be there for you, Abbie. I want to stand by your side."

Abbie's breath caught in her throat, her eyes shimmering with a mix of surprise and gratitude at Simon's unexpected confession. She felt a surge of warmth, a flicker of renewed hope in the wake of their fractured connection.

"Simon, I-" Abbie started, but her words faltered as she struggled to articulate the swell of emotions within her.

Simon took a step closer, releasing her arm but still standing close, his gaze unwavering as he spoke with a newfound determination.

"I don't know how, but I'll figure it out. I'll find a way to make things right, to help you. Just... give me the chance, Abbie."

In one sweeping stride, Simon closed the gap between them. In a moment of ale-fueled courage, he pressed his lips against hers, the tenderness of the gesture catching Abbie off-guard. As they shared a tentative kiss, the air was electric with an unspoken promise of renewed trust and a budding affection between them.

As their lips parted, Abbie gazed at Simon, the intensity of his golden eyes sending a shiver down her spine. In an unspoken declaration, Simon wrapped his arms around her, pulling her close in a protective embrace, his voice a mere whisper.

"...can we lay together again tonight?"

As Simon's words lingered in the air, the warmth of his arms enveloped her, their bodies fitting together like two halves of a whole. The flickering candlelight bathed them in a muted glow, casting their shadows in an intimate embrace. Their breaths mingled in the silence of the tavern, a moment of shared understanding passing between them.

As Simon held her close, Abbie felt a newfound security, a sense of safety in the midst of uncertainty. In his arms, she knew she could weather the coming storm.

She buried her face in the crook of his neck, breathing in the scent of him- earthy, warm, and comforting. Her heart was at peace, nestled against his.

"Of course, Simon," Abbie whispered, her lips grazing his neck with the faintest hint of a kiss. "I'd like that."

He parted, an anxious excitement buzzing through his veins. He tossed a few coins onto the counter.

"One night," He said, and was handed a key to the rooms upstairs.

WITH A SOFT SMILE, Simon took her hand and led her upstairs, their fingers interlaced as the candlelight cast their shadows in a dance of devotion and anticipation.

"Abbie," Simon started, his voice soft and sincere. "I... I don't know how we're going to do this. But I want to be here for you, every step of the way. If you'll let me."

Abbie met his gaze, a sense of wonder and gratitude filling her heart at his earnest offer.

"I don't know how, either," she admitted. "But I'd like that, Simon. Very much."

As they stepped into the room, the light of the moon bathed them in a silver glow, illuminating the bond between them-a connection that transcended the fracture of trust and the trials that lay ahead.

Their lips met in a passionate kiss, the world fell away, their hearts united as one.

And in that moment, all was right in the world.

Abbie wrapped her arms around Simon's neck, her body flush against his. Her pulse quickened, a wave of heat washing over her as the intensity of his touch ignited a fire within her. Simon's hands trailed along her back, his fingers caressing her skin as he deftly undid the clasps of her dress. As the fabric fell away, exposing her bare skin to the cool night air, Abbie shivered, both from the chill and the anticipation of Simon's touch.

He lowered her onto the bed, his hands exploring the curves of her body with reverence. As he worshipped her with his lips, she arched into him, her hips moving in time with his as they explored each other in a sensual rhythm.

The tension between them built with every kiss, every touch, until Abbie was aching with need.

"Simon," she breathed, her voice barely a whisper.

With a low growl, Simon buried his face in the crook of her neck, his teeth grazing her skin. As he bit down, the sweet sting of his canines pierced her flesh, his mouth hungrily marking her. The pleasure-pain mix of his bite sent Abbie over the edge, her body writhing beneath his as she cried out his name. Her head spun, the world around her fading away as the intensity of the moment overwhelmed her senses.

She wiggled beneath him, squirming until she managed to find the perfect opportunity. When he came up for another desperate breath, she hungrily kissed him, and then rolled him over and mounted him.

They both paused, and for a moment, nothing but the sound of their labored breaths and racing hearts could be heard as she sat in his lap, feeling his stiffness against the back of her thigh.

She slowly moved, her hips grinding against him. He grabbed her waist, guiding her as they found their rhythm.

"C-can I..." He whimpered, already hard and throbbing for release.

"Not yet," she whispered back, and a smirk crept up her face.

She continued, agonizingly slow, and he threw his head back, his chest rising and falling rapidly.

"Oh, Gods, Abbie..."

"I told you, not yet."

He groaned, but nodded, his body quivering with pleasure.

With every movement, he was brought closer to the edge, his breathing becoming more erratic. He gripped her hips tightly, his fingers digging into her flesh.

"Please," he begged, his voice barely a whisper.

Her pace increased, her body aching for release.

"Not yet."

Their bodies moved together, their breaths mingling as they surrendered to the moment.

Eventually, she couldn't hold back her desire for him. Simon clearly wasn't very experienced, and neither was she- but she'd had more than a few rendezvous with the village boys that had so graciously declared themselves nude models for her to sketch. Some experience was better than none, and she took pride in the little tricks she had learned along the way.

She knew how to make a man melt, and what better way to make things up to him?

"Simon... Simon, I want you."

He shuddered, a low growl emanating from his throat. He sat up and pulled her further into his lap, her legs wrapping around his waist. He held her tightly, his fingers tangling in her hair as he gazed into her eyes.

"Abbie," he whispered, his voice laced with a mixture of adoration and desperation.

With a deep breath, she shifted her hips and guided him inside her. She gasped, her eyes widening at the sensation.

"Is this okay?" he murmured, his eyes searching hers for any sign of discomfort.

"Yes," she breathed, her arms tightening around his neck. "Oh, yes."

She began to move, her hips rocking in a slow, steady rhythm. He clutched her tightly, his body trembling as she took control. Her walls tightened around his thick, throbbing shaft, driven by the instinct to please him.

They moved together, their bodies connected in a dance of pleasure and passion. They were lost in the moment, consumed by each other's touch, the rest of the world falling away.

He panted between gentle kisses on her neck and the moans that escaped his lips. He struggled to hold back his wolf, who for the first time, was firm in his desire- he wanted her, he wanted her to be *his*.

With each passing second, the pressure inside them built, their bodies seeking release. As their movements became more urgent, their lips met in a searing kiss, the intensity of the moment pushing them over the edge.

"Please, Simon..."

Hearing her moan his name made a soft, pleased growl rumble from deep within him. He crashed his lips into hers before he flipped their position, asserting himself on top. His soft hands now firmly gripping her wrists, holding them tightly above her head.

The pressure building up inside of her was growing rapidly. He knew that she was getting closer and closer, and the feeling was intoxicating.

He was determined to get her there, to give her everything that he could.

The sight of her below him, panting and moaning, was enough to make him almost lose control. His grip on her wrists tightened as his thrusts became harder and faster, his own release drawing closer.

"Don't stop," she begged, her voice a breathless whisper. "Oh, Simon, that feels so good..."

With a growl, Simon buried his face in the crook of her neck, his teeth grazing her skin, leaving more marks across her pale flesh. His rhythm became erratic, his hips bucking wildly as he reached his climax. Abbie arched her back, her body quaking as waves of pleasure washed over her. Simon's body trembled as his own orgasm overtook him, their bodies shuddering in unison as they rode out the aftershocks of their mutual pleasure.

Simon's weight rested on top of her, their bodies pressed together in a heated tangle of limbs. He buried his face in the crook of her neck, his breath warm on her skin as he struggled to catch his breath.

Abbie's fingers traced patterns across his back, her heartbeat slowing as the euphoria of the moment faded. He gently stroked her hair, his lips brushing against her forehead.

"I think I'm falling for you, Abbie," he confessed, his voice barely a whisper.

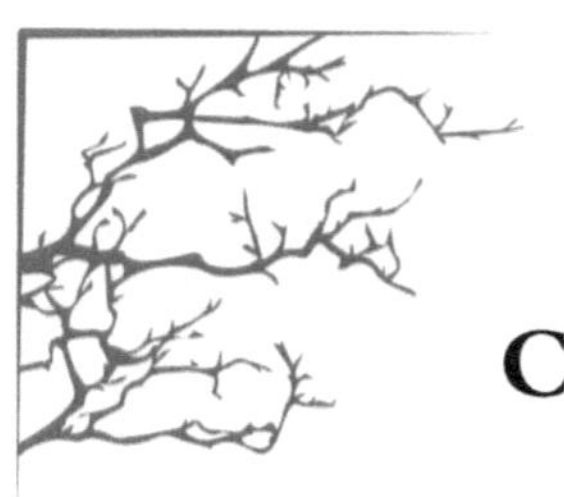

Chapter Thirteen

"E asy now, easy..."
Jett tried to tell himself over and over to relax as his vision blurred. He could barely make out the buildings in front of him, let alone think of what he was supposed to do. He had a task, a job ahead- but none of it seemed to matter now.

His grip was slipping.

He had always been one to try to suppress his spirit-side. In fact, while most of those lucky enough to be born as a werewolf- or even better, an Alpha like Tamsen- enjoyed the raw freedom that an animal form gave, he hated the little bastard he was forever bound to.

He'd learned early on that with enough practice, the curse could be kept at bay. With enough knowledge of runes, one could lock themselves in human form, at the turmoil of the other soul.

Constant urges, ticks, and uncontrollable outbursts had long ago been stamped out into nothing but a cold, emotionless exterior.

But Abbie had changed all that.

He was breaking.

He ducked into an alley as his knees gave way beneath him.

Just out of sight, just in time.

The first sign of his transformation manifested in subtle tremors coursing through his frame, a quivering sensation that rippled beneath his skin like an untamed tempest longing to break free from its confines. His hands, once steady, now convulsed involuntarily, fingers elongating into darkened talons.

He stripped his jacket, hearing the soft clang of the blades within. He tried to stuff it somewhere hidden- behind a stack of worn wooden crates- rushing to stash it before he no longer had the blessing of opposable thumbs.

With a guttural cry that echoed through the hushed night, Jett's form contorted and shifted, bones and sinew reshaping themselves in a cataclysmic upheaval. Feathers sprouted from his skin, black as midnight yet iridescent in the moon's ethereal glow. His flesh melded and twisted, birthing wings that unfurled with an ominous grace.

His face contorted, elongating into a sharp, beak-like visage, a fusion of human and raven features that held an unsettling allure. Eyes that once held a predatory confidence now gleamed with an otherworldly intensity, twin orbs of onyx that seemed to peer into the depths of one's soul.

The air crackled with energy as Jett, now a magnificent raven, took flight with a haunting caw that echoed through the night.

"DUMB FUCKER. HOW MANY blades do you think he's got?"

"Too many," Another man growled.

"Wanna bet?" The first one- the one who wore the Mage armor that reeked with the scent of dried blood- chuckled. "I bet less than ten. If we find more on his body, I'll buy you a drink."

"Deal."

In the recesses of the dimly lit alley, Tamsen stood, his senses keen and attuned to the conversation unfolding nearby. His posture, once relaxed, stiffened with apprehension as he overheard the intentions of the shadowy figure. Their plot to meet Jett, intending to murder him and seize the coveted Arcane weapons, ignited a furious blaze within Tamsen.

"You plan to kill him, do you?" Tamsen's voice, normally steady and composed, crackled with a raw, ferocious edge as he stepped forward.

Startled, the figure spun around, their features obscured by the cloak of darkness.

"Who the hell are you? Stay out of this!" they retorted, attempting to mask their growing alarm with false bravado.

A snarl curled Tamsen's lips as an ominous transformation surged through him. His body convulsed as bones elongated and muscles rippled, shifting him into a fearsome werewolf, a creature of primal might and untamed fury.

The figure drew a concealed dagger, their eyes alight with malice.

"Stupid dog! I'll deal with you first, and then I'll take what I came for!" they spat, lunging forward with deadly intent.

Tamsen's reflexes were honed to a razor-sharp edge. Before the blade could be plunged into his flesh, the werewolf's massive claws swept up, ripping through the man's arm. Blood gushed from the wound, spurting across the ground in a crimson river as the man cried out in agonized shock.

"I'll show you who's a stupid dog, bastard," the werewolf snarled, his voice distorted with rage.

"What the hell is that thing?!" another shadowy figure, the one who had placed the bet, exclaimed, horrified.

"Kill it!" the first one gasped, clutching at his profusely bleeding arm.

Before Tamsen could strike again, the second figure produced an arrow, nocking it in a fluid, practiced motion and loosing it toward the werewolf. The missile whistled through the air, striking Tamsen in the shoulder, the sharpened flint boring deep into the muscle.

"Call the city guard!" the man ordered, his voice wavering. "They'll handle this beast!"

"Go ahead and run," Tamsen growled, his eyes gleaming in the dark. "You won't make it far. Not now, not ever."

With a bestial roar, the werewolf lunged forward, his claws slashing at the fleeing men. The scent of fresh blood mingled with the stench of fear, driving Tamsen into a frenzy. His claws tore through the air, shredding the figures in a whirlwind of destruction.

The man with the injured arm was the first to fall, his body riddled with deep gashes and vicious bite wounds. As his lifeblood seeped from his body, he attempted to scream, only to be cut off by a massive claw ripping through his neck, nearly severing his head from his shoulders.

His partner didn't fare any better. Even as he scrambled away from the crazed monster, a heavy paw slammed into his back, knocking him to the ground. The wolf's fangs sank into his leg, crunching bone and sinew before finishing with a vicious twist. Pain shock took the man in an instant. His vision went white as the agony of a shattered leg flooded his system.

As quickly as it had begun, the carnage was over.

Reverting to his human form, Tamsen stood amidst the aftermath, his chest heaving with exertion. The stolen mage armor lay discarded, a stark reminder of the dire confrontation that had just transpired. Though a sense of relief washed over him for having thwarted the sinister plot, a haunting sorrow lingered in his gaze.

"Fuck, fuck, fuck..."

He had always been protective over Jett and Simon. He had to be. He had to be the strong one, the one who always had it together, the one who always knew what to do.

But now, his hands- *still slick with blood*- trembled at his sides. He reached up, tentatively touching the arrow still lodged in his flesh. He closed his eyes, biting his lip as he gripped it, before pulling it out with a swift yank. Blood trickled down his exposed chest, and he wanted to scream, but he refused to make a sound.

There wasn't any hiding it.

And there was no way he'd get the group out of the city in time.

Swiftly responding to the disturbance, the guards rushed towards the source of the commotion, their armored footsteps echoing ominously against the cobblestone streets.

Panic swept through him. He had to make a move.

A surge of adrenaline fueled his movements as he dashed into the labyrinthine network of alleys, using his familiarity with the city's nooks and crannies to his advantage. The guards arrived at the scene, their voices clamoring in confusion as they surveyed the aftermath of the confrontation- a discarded cloak and remnants of arcane armor lay strewn about crimson pools and painted walls.

The city guards, alerted and determined, fanned out in pursuit, their torchlights casting eerie flickers against the looming buildings.

Tamsen navigated through the narrow passageways with the agility of a hunted predator, his footsteps silent as he melted into the shadows, evading the probing gaze of the guards. Each alley he traversed brought him closer to eluding capture, his heart pounding in tandem with the rhythm of his swift escape.

As the echoes of his footsteps faded into the nocturnal symphony, Tamsen disappeared from sight, leaving behind only the whispers of his elusive presence.

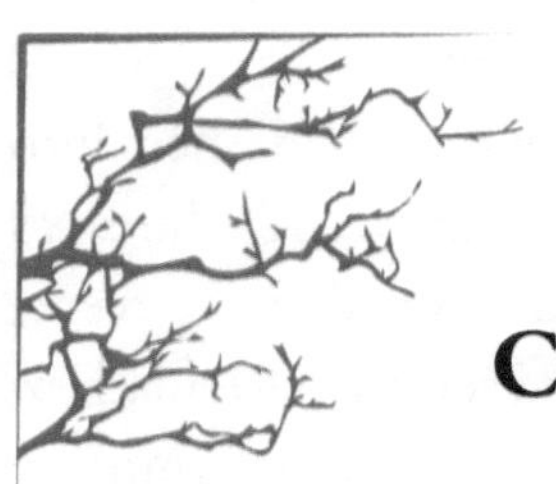

Chapter Fourteen

In the aftermath of his transformation, Jett found himself enveloped in the embrace of his raven form. His senses, now attuned to the whims of the night, guided him through the city streets. The moon, a silvery beacon in the sky, painted the buildings and cobblestone pathways below in a mystic luminescence.

Driven by instinct, Jett's avian eyes were drawn to glimmers and reflections that danced in the moonlight. His raven form possessed an inherent fascination with shiny objects, an innate allure that tugged at his feathered soul. The cityscape unfolded before him, a tapestry of shadows and secrets, each alleyway and rooftop holding the promise of hidden treasures.

As he swooped and glided over the city, his keen gaze caught a flicker of light emanating from a cobblestone pathway below. Descending gracefully, his ebony wings slicing through the air with an otherworldly elegance, Jett landed upon the ground.

There, nestled amidst the stones, lay a lost ring- its metallic surface gleaming in the moon's soft radiance.

In an instant, a decision was made- this precious find would be a token of his affection for Abbie, the girl who held the heart of both souls trapped within.

With the glimmering ring gently clutched in his talons, Jett embarked on his mission.

As Jett approached the bustling tavern, the warm glow of lamplight spilled out onto the cobbled street, contrasting with the night's cool exterior. The scent of ale and roasted meats wafted through the air, mingling with laughter and lively conversation that echoed from within.

The raven perched upon a nearby ledge, observing the comings and goings through the tavern's open doors and shuttered windows. He scanned the dimly lit interior, seeking the familiar face of Abbie amidst the eclectic mix of patrons.

However, she was nowhere to be found among the revelers.

With a sense of urgency fueled by his unwavering determination, Jett decided to take matters into his own talons.

Ignoring the curious gazes of passersby, he ventured into the tavern, his ebony feathers a striking contrast against the warm, wooden interior.

As he gracefully glided into the establishment, a hush fell over the patrons. The unexpected appearance of a raven within the tavern's confines elicited a chorus of murmurs and gasps, mingled with exclamations of disbelief. Conversations tapered off, and curious eyes followed the bird's every movement.

At least, shifters like him were rare.

Werewolves had once colonized the Fyrean kingdom, but were pushed out as the area by the Caeds many ages ago. When their kind- once spread out vast over the kingdom's lands- were forced to funnel into the dense wilderness at the fringes of what lay charted, some unexpected mutations ran amok through the shifter's population.

Jett, undeterred by the attention he attracted, maintained his focus on his mission. His keen gaze darted from table to table, searching for the one person he'd caw for.

Amidst the flickering candlelight and the mingled scents of ale and hearth, the patrons exchanged bewildered glances, unable to comprehend how a raven had ventured into their midst. Some whispered tales of superstition, others regarded the bird with a mixture of awe and trepidation, while a few attempted to shoo it away, believing it to be an ill omen.

Undaunted, Jett continued his meticulous search, fluttering from perch to perch, a raven on a quest driven for affection. He perched atop a wooden beam, his piercing gaze scanning the room, desperately hoping to catch sight of the golden blonde curls amongst the crowd.

But as the minutes stretched into hours, there was still no sign of Abbie. The fervent desire to gift her the lost ring, now morphed into a sense of frustration tinged with worry. He swooped down from his vantage point, landing on the bearskin rug before the fireplace. With little bird steps, he hopped towards the stairs, disappearing around the corner.

Maybe she'd already gotten a room and gone to bed?

His ebony feathers shimmered in the faint glow that filtered through the hallway's sconces, each step marked by an air of determination. With a swift grace, he perched on doorknobs, a silent sentinel peering through keyholes into the intimate sanctuaries of the inn's chambers. His keen avian gaze scanned each room, yearning for the sight of Abbie, hoping to find her within the embrace of the inn's quarters.

Room after room offered nothing but shadows and empty spaces. Each vacant scene felt like a cruel echo of disappointment, a crescendo of apprehension building within the raven's breast.

Yet, fate seemed to unveil a bittersweet revelation behind the third door he inspected.

Through the keyhole's aperture, a scene unfolded- Abbie nestled in an embrace with Simon.

The boy Jett had grown up with.

The one who had been at his side, through thick and thin.

He had a protective arm wrapped around her waste, their silhouettes were bathed in the soft, flickering glow of candlelight.

In that suspended moment, time seemed to fracture for the raven-turned-Jett.

Betrayal etched its mark upon the raven's essence, fracturing the fragile illusion of affection and trust. His glossy feathers seemed to quiver, and a soft, sad call escaped his throat. Each breath seemed laden with sorrow as the raven struggled to reconcile the whirlwind of emotions. Hurt and disbelief mingled within the depths of his avian soul, a tempest that threatened to consume him whole.

With a tentative flutter of wings, the raven began to depart, its dark form a fleeting shadow against the moonlit corridor. Yet, even as it poised to flee, an unsettling wave of desolation and despair swept through the avian spirit. A profound emptiness gnawed at the very core of its being, a yearning for solace amidst the ache of betrayal.

In an abrupt whirlwind of transformation, the raven's sleek feathers shimmered and shifted. Bones contorted beneath his skin, muscles quivered with raw energy as the ethereal dance between human and avian form unfurled.

JETT AWOKE ON THE GROUND in his human form. He groaned, sitting up before hazily glancing around him.

Something was different.

For the first time...

He couldn't feel his spirit-side.

The link to his raven seemed now tethered to nothing, ,and any calls to it were like echoes in the abyss.

Jett stood in the dimly lit corridor, his chest heaving with ragged breaths. The abrupt shift from avian to human left him disoriented, his senses reeling from the abrupt transition.

Yet, his icy demeanor shattered as the memories came flooding back. His fists clenched involuntarily, nails digging into his palms, a storm brewed within his human frame- a tempest of rage and jealousy that threatened to engulf him whole. The revelation of betrayal, the sight that had shattered the delicate fabric of trust and affection, ignited an inferno of emotions within his chest.

Abbie was his, and no one else's.

The time for caution had passed.

He didn't need Simon or Tamsen.

They'd just get in the way of him and Abbie.

He'd take her to the castle himself. Then, he'd save Iris. He'd drive his favorite blade right through the King's heart before flaying the rest of the Caeds alive.

He'd do it all for her.

And, if they wanted- he'd *happily* let the sisters participate in the torture he had planned, a well-earned revenge was always his favorite treat.

Then, Abigail would have no choice but to fall for him...

Just as he had fallen for her.

"It's my turn now, Simon," Jett muttered under his breath, his eyes gleaming with a dangerous glint. "Time to take what's mine."

He paused outside her door.

With a deep breath, he turned the knob and entered the room, his eyes locking on her sleeping form.

The sight of her, curled up on the bed, her soft breaths stirring the air, sent a surge of desire through him. He crept toward her, his steps silent, his fury bubbling beneath the surface.

He *had* to take her- get her far away from Simon's grubby little hands. She was his, and his alone. No one would come between them, no one would ever stand in his way.

He bent over her, his breath ghosting across her cheek.

"You're mine, Abbie," he whispered, his voice a dark promise. "Forever."

He slipped his arms under her and scooped her up, cradling her against his chest.

"*Mine.*"

With a final glance at Simon's slumbering form, he slipped out of the room, his precious cargo tucked safely in his arms.

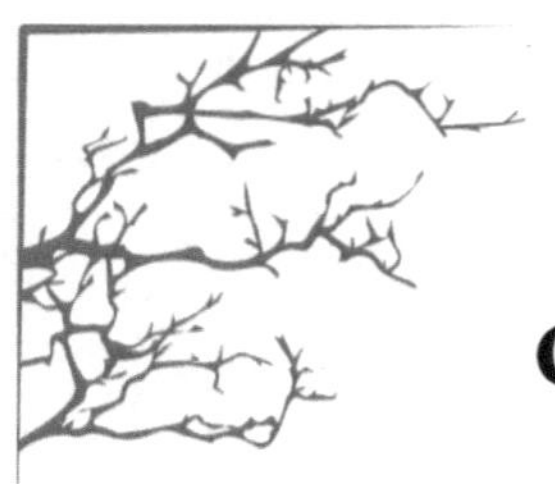

Chapter Fifteen

S imon awoke with a start, the warmth of slumber slowly fading as he reached out for Abbie in the darkness, only to grasp at emptiness. His brow furrowed in confusion before his eyes fluttered open, adjusting to the dimly lit room of the inn they had rented for the night.

The room was small and quaint, illuminated by the soft glow of a single flickering candle resting on a wooden table beside the bed. The walls, made of sturdy stone, bore the marks of age with ivy creeping through small cracks, lending a rustic charm to the place. The bed itself was a sturdy wooden frame with a simple mattress, adorned with a few blankets and furs to ward off the night's chill.

As Simon's consciousness fully returned, a sense of unease washed over him.

"Abbie?" His voice was hoarse, tinged with sleep, as he called out her name into the silence, the only response being the faint crackling of the dying embers in the fireplace.

Hastily throwing off the covers, he swung his legs over the edge of the bed, his bare feet meeting the cool, rough surface of the stone floor beneath him. He stumbled forward, a sense of urgency guiding his movements as he called out for her once more.

"Abbie!" His voice echoed down the empty hallway, the sound bouncing off the ancient walls.

There was no answer.

He rushed out of the room, down the hallway, and into the courtyard.

"ABBIE!" Simon's desperate cry pierced the silence, his heart pounding in his chest. The name echoed through the stone corridors, bouncing off the walls in a haunting chorus.

Yet, there was no response.

"Abbie?"

His heart stopped.

She was gone.

His breaths grew shallow as he stumbled forward, his frantic search leading to an agonizing realization. Abbie was nowhere to be found. His mate, his *everything*, had vanished without a trace.

Simon sank to his knees, tears streaming down his cheeks.

"Please, Gods," he prayed, his voice barely a whisper. "Please, let her be okay."

TAMSEN LEANED BACK against the stone wall, lingering in the alley behind the tavern. He still held his bleeding shoulder, the shock beginning to wear, so he could experience all the joys of an arrow wound.

He could smell the tang of blood, the iron scent filling his nostrils.

And his fangs...

His canines throbbed, his mouth salivating.

It had been so long since he'd given his wolf a taste of blood, but boy, did it feel *good*.

And the adrenaline was still pumping through his veins.

But he was injured, and he was vulnerable.

Then, he smelled something familiar.

Someone.

Someone he knew.

"Simon..." He groaned, pushing himself off the wall.

He stumbled forward, his eyes scanning the streets.

Then, he spotted him.

Simon was running, his eyes frantic, his face a mask of fear.

Tamsen watched, his vision blurring slightly.

"Simon!" His voice was strained, and the words barely made it out of his throat.

But Simon stopped, and turned. Their eyes met, and the world seemed to stop spinning.

"Tamsen, are you alright?" Simon asked, rushing towards him.

"I've been better," Tamsen replied, his voice weak.

"You're bleeding," Simon said, his jaw hanging open.

"No shit," Tamsen muttered, his vision swimming. "We might have...a problem..."

"Here, let me help you," Simon said, putting his arm around Tamsen's waist. The Alpha almost stumbled, but then, he seemed to find his footing again. He glanced around, trying to find something he could...use.

He needed magic.

And magic needed a fuel.

Shit. There's not even a stray cat nearby?

"Thanks," Tamsen said, his eyes meeting Simon's.

"I have to find Abbie," Simon said, his face filled with concern.

"I'll help you," Tamsen said, his grip tightening on Simon's shoulder. "Where'd you last see her?"

In the haze of his desperation to find her, Simon let his secret slip.

"She was in my bed, and then-"

"She *what*?" Tamsen hissed, his eyes blazing.

"I didn't do anything, she's not like that," Simon said, his voice panicked. Without even looking at him- falling apart beneath the seams, his anxiety consuming him at the accusation- Tamsen could *smell* the lie on his lips. "We were just sleeping. She's... My mate."

The words hung heavy in the air.

Tamsen's wolf howled in frustration, in pain.

"You're not her mate," he said, his voice low.

He was lying.

He had to be.

Right?

"Tamsen, I'm sorry. I didn't mean to-"

"Fuck you," Tamsen snarled, pushing away from Simon.

"Tamsen, please," Simon begged, reaching for him.

"You think you can have her? You think you deserve her? You're just a coward, hiding behind your books and the good boy act. She needs a real man, someone who can protect her," Tamsen spat, his claws digging into his palms. "Not a weasely brat who thinks he can overstep his Alpha!"

A bitter idea crossed his mind.

Something he never thought he was capable to think.

Even through the pain, he grabbed Simon by the back of his shirt. His hand snapped up and then grabbed his neck, the act of dominance making the Beta's body lock in fear.

"T-t-tamsen!" He cried in alarm.

Tamsen's eyes blazed with a fury he had never seen before. A low growl rumbled from his chest, and Simon could feel the tiny, electric pinpricks erupting from Tamsen's warming hands.

Magic.

Arcane Magic.

Simon tried to scream, but was cut off as he felt his energy fading, his neck beginning to burn.

"Tamsen, w-wait! Don't-"

"Shhhh..."

Tamsen's voice was soothing, almost hypnotic, as he pressed his clawed thumb against Simon's lips.

"Don't struggle. It'll be over soon."

Simon whimpered as he felt the last of his strength leave him.

The air was thick with the smell of blood and magic.

"P-please..." Simon begged, his eyes fluttering shut.

And with that, Simon's eyes closed, his body falling limp in Tamsen's arms.

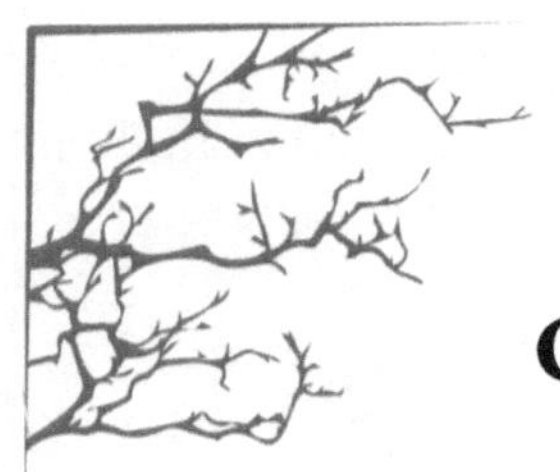

Chapter Sixteen

The next morning, Abbie woke up disoriented. Her head was pounding, her limbs weak and shaky. The night before came rushing back, the memory of the heated kiss, the feeling of Simon's hands on her bare skin.

She looked around, her gaze falling on Jett's sleeping form.

What the fuck?

She studied him, her heart clenching at the sight of him.

No, no.

She had a few drinks, then went to bed with *Simon...*

Her memory flickered with the heat of the passionate kisses, the melody of his moans, and the tingle of his breath on her neck.

There was no way she'd do that with Jett.

She shook her head, trying to clear the fogginess. Her eyes darted around the room, landing on her clothing, folded neatly on the chair beside her.

With a start, she realized that she was completely naked, the sheets wrapped tightly around her. She clutched them to her chest, her mind reeling.

How did I get here?

And where was Simon?

Her stomach twisted with fear and anxiety.

"Oh, Gods," she whispered, her voice trembling.

She glanced at Jett, his chest rising and falling with each steady breath. There was no signs of trouble, no signs of wrongdoing. Had he made an unwanted move on her, she surely would've clawed his eyes out...

But no.

Everything said that she had wanted it.

Her cheeks turned a deep cherry red as she shook off the thought.

She had to get out of here.

Now.

She slowly crept out of bed, her legs shaky as she reached for her clothes. She dressed hastily, her hands fumbling with the buttons, her heart racing.

"Come on, come on," she muttered, her voice barely a whisper.

Once fully clothed, she tiptoed to the door, her hand trembling as she reached for the handle.

"I didn't give you permission to leave," A cold voice bellowed from behind her. "Where do you think you're going, Darling?"

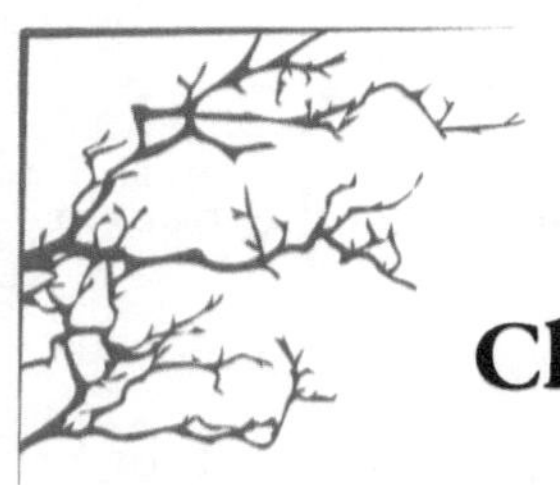

Chapter Seventeen

"I...I'm sorry," she stammered, her voice wavering. "I didn't mean to wake you."

"Come here."

His voice was low and dangerous, and there was no doubt in her mind that his words were nothing short of a demand. She flinched, torn between her defiance and the urge to make things go smoothly by simply obeying. Still, the thought of Iris lingered in her mind. She'd already wasted time, too much time, and she had to get moving soon.

"I...I'm sorry, I really have to go. My sister-"

"I said, come. *Here.*"

Abbie flinched at the harshness of his tone, her stomach churning with dread.

She took a deep breath and turned to face him.

"I'm sorry. I think I got confused last night. Please, can we talk about this later?"

"Later?" He cocked his head, a cruel smile twisting his lips. "There is no later. Come on, lay back down, I'll bring you breakfast. We'll start over, properly."

"No, really, I'm fine." She backed away from him, her hands held up in defense. "Please, Jett. I have to find Simon."

"Simon?" His expression darkened, his eyes narrowing to slits, the name almost a curse on his tongue.

"Yes," She said, although she wasn't sure of herself.

Had she really been with Simon? Sure, she wasn't the type to pass up an opportunity, but sleeping with two guys seemed like a bit of a stretch- no pun intended.

"*Why* do you want to find him?

"Because..." She searched for the words.

What the hell am I supposed to say?

"Because what?"

"I don't know," she said, her voice barely above a whisper.

"You don't know why you want to find Simon?"

"I...I..." Her hand was still on the cold handle of the door. Jett stepped forward, smoothly closing the gap between them. He let out a frustrated sigh, but then he wrapped his arms around her, burying his warm face into her neck.

"Abbie, please," He whispered. "I just..."

He hugged her tighter, and his breath hitched ever-so-slightly.

"...I just don't want to be alone anymore."

She froze, her heart fluttering in her chest.

What the hell was that?

"Jett..."

He sighed and pulled away, turning to stare out the window.

"Don't leave. Just...just stay."

"...fine," She conceded. "I'll stay. But where's Tamsen?"

"He should be back soon," He took her hands in his own, kissing her halm gently. "Please. Sit down. I'll make us something to eat, and then we'll hit the road when he gets back."

She reluctantly nodded, settling into the small wooden table in the room.

Jett moved with a quiet yet assured grace, his hands expertly maneuvering amidst the pots and pans in the inn's makeshift kitchen. The clinking of utensils, the sizzle of food upon the stove- a symphony of culinary expertise orchestrated by a man driven by an inexplicable determination- filled the room, along with a myriad of mouthwatering smells.

Before her eyes, a scene unfolded- even despite the limited kitchen, a breakfast that bordered on extravagance laid out before her. The aroma of freshly brewed tea mingled with the scent of sizzling bacon, the vibrant colors of fruits and pastries teasing the senses with their enticing allure. A cornucopia of flavors, meticulously arranged with an artist's precision, adorned the table- a feast crafted from the heart.

"I couldn't go through with the sale," Jett confessed, his voice a blend of earnestness and conviction. "When I went back for my jacket, the guy I was supposed to meet was gone. Nobody else wanted to talk to me, and the guards were sniffing around. Took a little walk in the market district. I had to... acquire some food. A necessity, given the circumstances."

Despite the tension that lingered between them, Jett's attempt to please her seemed to eclipse the unease. He moved with a deliberate grace, setting the table with a serene determination that hinted at a desire to set things right, to pave a new path forward.

As Abbie sat, her gaze fixed upon the lavish feast before her, a jumble of emotions danced behind her eyes- confusion, concern, and a flicker of uncertainty mingled within the depths of her gaze.

Her mind whirled, the memory of his hands roaming her body, his lips on hers, the taste of him, the smell of him, all came crashing back.

"Did...did we...?" She gestured between them.

He stared at her, his dark eyes pools of bitter emotions- love, jealousy, desire, and loneliness, all wrapped up into the bad boy mask he put on for the world. His eyes searched hers for signs of regret, signs of guilt, or if her feelings mirrored his own.

"Would you be against it if we did?" He asked, hurt leaking into his words.

She hesitated, the truth burning her lips.

Would she?

It didn't mattter, at the end of the day. She'd already come to terms with that, ever since the day she'd heard the news as to why the mages had rejected her examination.

The days had been a blur. One morning, she had dolled herself up for the arrival of the younger Prince Alexios, who desired a blood-slave from her village. She hadn't even told Iris. Nobody but her best friend, Hanna, had a clue of her intentions.

Hanna wasn't far behind, her round face grinning in the mirror as she pressed the goldthread dress against her body. She rearranged the dark triple-braided bundle of hair that was intertwined with various flowers she had begged Abbie's mother to pick for her. She had made a dumb excuse- visiting the grave of a non-existant dead relative had been enough to convince her mom to pick all of the butterscotch roses she could find.

Had either of their parents known what they were signing up for, they would've stopped it in a heartbeat.

"You think this one will look okay?' She asked, her voice a timid murmur.

"Girl, you're fine. More fine than me," Abbie replied, taking a moment to fret over her long blonde hair in the mirror. "I barely got any sleep last night. I look like shit."

"You're too hard on yourself, Abbie. I'm sure you got this."

"Whatever you say," Abbie replied, straightening her hair.

An uncomfortable silence passed between them before Hanna spoke up, voicing the thought that was on both of their minds.

"You sure you're ready for this?" Hanna said. "What if we actually get picked?"

Abigail paused for a moment. Part of the contract meant that the rest of her family would be taken care of, and even education costs for members of the family would be paid for by the Crown. She had hoped that they'd consider letting her sister have a shot at the Academy, but she wouldn't mind what school she got to go to, so long as she got the training she deserved.

As much as she should have been afraid of what the vampires would do to her, the thought brought her an odd sense of anticipation. She had always been the type to prefer a bad boy, but she could only imagine the types of things the coldhearted monsters planned to do to their toys. The allure of a life far away from the village was tempting enough, and if she was selected, she wouldn't have to feel any guilt, because everything back home would be taken care of.

"Then, when we get to the castle and live like Princesses," She said with a smile, despite the inexplicable dull ache of pain in her abdomen. Something she had been meaning to get checked out, but never got around to. Now, she'd get an even better examination, from the best mages the Kingdom had to offer. "I'm stealing all of the pound cake and you can't stop me."

"Such blasphemy," Hanna giggled. "As a future Royal Princess, you should watch your tongue!"

The two laughed, their friendship keeping the two together, even through the uncertainty of the future.

"STEP FORWARD."

"Oh, Gods," Hanna whispered, reaching out to clasp Abbie's hand, desperate for some sort of reassurance. "We're next..."

"It's gonna be a piece of cake," Abbie replied, squeezing her hand in an attempt to soothe her. "Pound cake, to be precise."

Hanna smiled softly.

"Thank you, Abbie. For being here. For me."

"Don't sweat it, you sappy idiot," Abbie retorted as she did some last-minute fixing of Hanna's hair. "You just go up there and you show them just how perfect you are for this."

She wasn't wrong.

Hanna's name was called, and with a last lingering glance, she uneasily walked towards the center of the town square. Past the dozens of onlookers, hooting and whistling, past the massive menacing horses bound to the Prince's caravan, and all the way to the center.

Right below the hungry gaze of the Prince.

"I like this one," He said with a smile. "Her friend, too. Be thorough on examining them both."

Three cloaked figures, dressed head to toe in blue silken garbs, bowed before the Prince. In the gentle morning light, while small runes along the cuffs of their clothes glowed softly, before fading back to silver threads. Their cloaks billowed as they walked, or floated, Abbie couldn't tell- they looked like ghosts, specters caught between worlds.

She was mesmerized as one of them took Hanna's wrist.

And another took hers.

"NO NEED TO BE ANXIOUS," A woman's voice soothed from beneath the robes. "This is all routine, nothing to worry about."

Abbie hadn't even noticed that she'd been so tense that her fists were still clenched, her knuckles white. They had led her inside, allowing the examinations to take place in the town hall, which had been sealed off temporarily from the public. She had the whole space to herself, at least, but she was nervous about where they had taken Hanna.

"S-sorry," Abbie whispered.

"Now, take off your clothes and stand against the wall. Posture is important, but don't be too stiff. This will only take a minute, and if something doesn't feel right, you tell me right away and I'll stop, okay?"

She wasn't afraid of the examination.

She was afraid of the result.

She nodded, her hands trembling as she slipped off her dress. When the cold air of the room hit her skin, she shivered, goosebumps erupting all over her body. She flinched when she felt a warm hand on her back, all the while she struggled to focus on the thought of relaxing.

"It'll be over soon."

The woman was more than gentle, taking care to make sure everything went as smooth as possible. The smell of magic leaked into the air, stifling the dusty air, almost stealing the breath from her lungs.

And then...

Then came the pain.

A strangled cry rang out in the vast empty room.

She fell to her knees, just as the world faded around her.

"NO! I WON'T GO WITHOUT HER!"

Abbie's eyes stirred to life. Someone had clothed her once more, but the cold still slipped through the rough-hewn seams of what she'd been given. The blurry cobblestone ground came into view, her eyes hazy and unfocused. She was in the Mage's arms, her limp body jostled as she was carried outside.

"NO!"

Hanna's shrieks echoed through the town square as one of the other mages held her back tightly. The Prince watched in distaste, his arms crossed and his jaw set, his eyes flickering in annoyance at the scene before him.

"Shut her up, would you?" The Prince's voice barked. "Fuck, it's bad enough I have to leave such a beauty behind..."

"She needs surgery," The mage replied, although the edge to her tone said she clearly had no patience for the pompous Prince's woes. "I need another Mage to help me, but we have to work fast."

"Whatever you need," The Prince grumbled with a wave of his hand. "But don't say I'm not a benevolent Prince. I doubt my brother would be so kind."

"Thank you, Your Highness," The mage muttered as Abbie's body was hoised onto one of the horses. She then mounted with a sigh, nudging the

steed with her heel. She assumed Abbie was still unconscious, and she just continued to vent to herself. "What a bitch he is. I bet if he was the one who got the news he wouldn't be able to have kids, he'd be singing a different tune..."

What?

The words barely sank into her barely conscious state.

SHE WOKE UP IN A ROOM she didn't recognize.

It was clean, and comfortable, for the most part. Enchanted blossoms sat by her bedside, and she was wrapped in the finest silk linens. It smelled lika a mix of tea tree and honey tea, with a subtle hint of magic lingering in the air.

Her head lulled to the side, and she caught sight of her mother. Her face was red, her eyes puffy, deep bags residing beneath them. After a moment of staring off at the wall, she noticed that her daughter was awake. She wiped her eyes on her sleeve before leaning down, giving Abigail a gentle kiss on the head.

"Abbie..." She said, her voice almost breaking. "Abigail, what were you thinking?"

"Mom, I..." Abbie looked away, her voice hoarse. She tried to move, but a wave of nausea washed over for her. Her breath caught in her throat when she looked down, seeing the bandage bound tightly around her waist.

"Don't move," Her mother said, a look of pain flickering in her eyes. "...you were sick, and we didn't know."

"S-sick?"

The words fell thickly on the room.

Neither of them spoke.

"My little darling..." She whispered finally, taking Abbie's hand in her own. "Let's keep today between us, shall we?"

Abbie nodded as tears welled in her eyes.

"WOULD YOU BE AGAINST it if we did?" He asked, hurt leaking into his words.

She hesitated, the truth burning her lips.

Would she?

It didn't mattter, at the end of the day. She'd already come to terms with that, ever since the day she'd heard the news as to why the mages had rejected her examination.

THE ANSWER WAS CLEAR.

"No, Jett. I wouldn't be against it."

He let out a long, shuddering breath, relief flooding his features. He turned away, his shoulders tense.

"Thank the Gods."

Abbie stood there, her head spinning, the room seeming to close in on her.

` "Jett, I-"

"Stay," he said, his voice firm.

She blinked, her mind reeling.

"Stay," he repeated. "Don't go, just...stay. Here. With me."

Her mouth was dry, her hands shaking. She didn't want to stay. She didn't want to get involved.

But...

Her mind flashed back to Simon's warm, tender touch. The feeling of being safe, of being cared for. The soft, gentle kisses that left her craving more.

But was it even real?

And if it wasn't...

Was it worth hurting Jett?

She took a deep breath, trying to steady herself.

"Okay," She said, her voice small.

He turned to her, his face illuminated by the early morning sun. He stepped towards her, his movements cautious and deliberate. He tilted her chin up, taking in the freckles that dotted her nose, the blush that lined her soft cheeks, and the glimmer of the morning rays in her amber eyes.

"Gods, you're beautiful," he whispered, his voice thick with emotion.

She blushed, the compliment sending warmth through her body.

"You're not so bad yourself," she said, a smile tugging at her lips.

In the quietude of the inn's morning, as the sun painted the room in a gentle golden hue. His hands trembled imperceptibly, betraying the weight of vulnerability beneath his composed exterior. With a solemn grace, he presented the ring he had found- the glint of its polished surface catching the sunlight as he placed it delicately in her palm.

"This ring... I found it amidst the fleeting shadows of the night," Jett began, his voice almost breaking. "It spoke of a story untold, a story I felt compelled to unravel."

"Jett..." She looked down at the ring, her eyes wide with wonder.

"I want my story to always be told with yours," He said, his words pleading. "I think I love you, Abbie."

He leaned in, pressing his lips to hers, the kiss full of desperation and longing. She melted into him, the feel of his lips against hers setting her soul aflame.

"Stay," he murmured, his lips brushing hers as he spoke.

He deepened the kiss, his tongue slipping into her mouth, his hands gripping her hips, pulling her flush against him. She moaned, the sound muffled by his kiss, her fingers digging into his back, his shoulders, anywhere she could reach.

"Please," he begged, his voice breaking.

"I'm staying," she gasped. "I'm not going anywhere."

His fingers slipped under her dress, his palms caressing her smooth skin. She shivered beneath him, arching into his warmth. He broke the kiss, his lips trailing down her jaw, her neck, his teeth grazing her skin.

"You're perfect," he murmured, his breath hot on her skin.

"Please," she whimpered, her body arching into his touch. "Jett, I want..."

"Want what?"

She whimpered, burying her face into his chest.

"...you."

He lifted her up, his strong arms holding her effortlessly, her legs wrapping around his waist. He carried her to the bed, gently laying her down. He kissed her again, his hands roaming her body, his touch setting her nerves on fire. She clung to him, her body aching for him, her need growing with every passing second.

"I need you," he breathed, his movements guided by nothing more than his desire for her. He could barely hold back, fighting the urge to ravage her, to claim her for his own.

"Take me," she whispered, her breath catching in her throat. He growled, his lips trailing down her neck, his teeth grazing her skin. He nipped at her collarbone, eliciting a gasp from her.

"Gods, I want you," he groaned, his voice low and husky. "I've wanted you since you first came to me..."

She shivered, the sound sending a thrill through her.

"I'm yours," she panted.

"You're mine," he echoed, his hands deftly removing her clothes, his fingers dipping into her folds.

She cried out, her body trembling with pleasure, his touch driving her wild.

"You're mine," he said again, his voice a possessive growl.

He stroked her, his thumb circling her clit, his fingers pumping into her. She writhed beneath him, her hips bucking against his hand.

"Oh, gods," she moaned, her breath ragged.

"You're mine," he repeated, his voice a deep, lustful whisper.

"Yours," she gasped, her body arching into him, her hands clutching the sheets, her eyes squeezed shut.

"*Mine*," he growled, again and again, his lips hovering over her ear. Every thrust of his hips made it clear how much he wanted her. She was his, and he was going to claim her, make her his own. The heat between her legs was building, her body trembling with the intensity of it. She could feel her orgasm approaching, and she clung to him, her fingers digging into his skin.

"Gods, Jett, I'm close," she moaned, her voice ragged.

"Come for me, Abbie," he demanded, his voice a low, seductive purr.

She cried out, her body tensing, her muscles contracting as the orgasm ripped through her. He continued to pump into her, prolonging her pleasure, his lips and teeth trailing along her neck.

"Oh, gods," she panted, her body shaking. "That felt..."

She was at a loss for words, her mind drawing a blank in the post-orgasm bliss. She hadn't come like that in...

Ever?

"I'm not done with you yet," he whispered, his fingers still working their magic.

She shivered, the thought of more sending a fresh wave of pleasure through her.

"Please," she begged, her voice hoarse. "I...I don't want you to stop...please...."

He chuckled, his eyes locked on hers, a wicked grin spreading across his lips.

"Mmm, you beg so prettily."

He kissed her, his lips rough and demanding. He plunged his fingers deeper into her, curling them and hitting her g-spot. She cried out, her body bucking against his hand, her legs trembling. His free hand pinned her arms above her head, with a firm grip that said she *certainly wasn't going anywhere.*

"More," she pleaded, her voice breathy.

"You want *more*?" He said, admiring her naked form. "Well, *Darling-* I think you're going to just have to be a good girl and earn it."

Abbie's heart pounded in her chest, her desire building to an almost painful level. She would do anything for him. *Anything.*

She swallowed, her mouth dry, her voice shaking as she spoke.

"Whatever you want."

Jett grinned, a look of triumph in his eyes.

"That's what I like to hear," he murmured.

He grabbed her, flipping her over so she was on her knees, her face buried in the sheets, her ass in the air. He ran his hands down her back, his fingers tracing her spine, sending a shiver down her body.

He pressed against her, his hard length teasing her entrance. She moaned, the sound muffled by the pillow, her hips grinding against him, desperate for his cock.

"Eager, are we?" He smirked, his voice full of amusement. "Stupid me, here I was thinking I'd have some convincing to do."

"Please," she gasped, her need growing by the second. She tried to push back, eager to feel him inside her. But he didn't give in easily, and he even gave her ass a hard smack for good measure. She whimpered, burying her face further into the sheets as the handprint reddened, her knees starting to tremble in desperation.

"You want this?" He teased, sliding the tip of his cock along her slit, her wetness coating him.

"Yes!"

"Tell me, Abbie. Tell me how much you want it."

"Gods, Jett," she groaned, her hips bucking, desperate for him. "Please, I want it. I need it."

"Beg me," he said, his voice a dark command.

"Please, Jett," she begged, her voice pleading. "Please fuck me."

He pushed into her, filling her, his hands gripping her hips, his pace steady. She moaned, the feeling of him inside her making her dizzy with desire.

"Gods, you're tight," he grunted, his fingers digging into her skin.

"More," she pleaded, her body craving his.

He quickened his pace, his cock slamming into her, his breath hot on her neck. She writhed beneath him, her climax building with each thrust.

"Fuck," he groaned, his teeth nipping her neck, his hands roaming her body, cupping her breasts, his fingers teasing her nipples.

"Yes, yes!" she cried, her body trembling.

"That's it," he growled, his voice a low, animalistic rumble. "Come for me, Abbie."

She felt her orgasm approach, the pleasure almost too much to bear. She gripped the sheets, her body quivering, the ecstasy washing over her in waves.

"Jett," she moaned, her climax sending her over the edge.

He thrust into her, his body tensing as he reached his peak. He let out a primal roar, his cock pulsing inside her, her inner walls clenching around him. They collapsed onto the bed, their bodies spent, their hearts pounding.

"Gods, you're amazing," he said, his voice full of awe.

"Mmm," she murmured, her eyes fluttering closed.

He wrapped his arms around her, holding her close, her body molded against his. As good as the romantic sex she'd had the night before was, the rough and dominating nature of Jett's fucking made her feel desired, wanted, and sexy.

She smiled, her mind hazy, her body tingling.

"Sleep, Abbie," Jett whispered, his lips brushing her ear. "Rest up. There's so much fun we're going to have together..."

She snuggled closer to him, her mind drifting, her body floating on a cloud of euphoria.

"I'm not letting you go," he said, his words barely registering in her consciousness.

She fell asleep in his arms, her heart full, her body sated.

For now, all was right with the world.

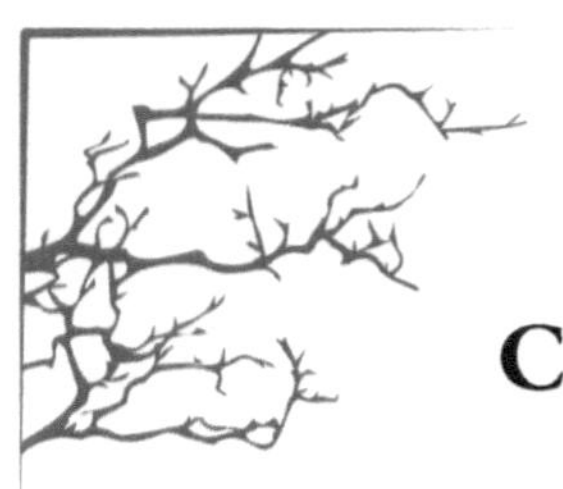

Chapter Eighteen

Simon's unconscious form lay in Tamsen's arms, a weight that felt both burdensome and strangely delicate. Tamsen's breath hitched as he gazed down at the Beta, his usual commanding aura replaced by a rare vulnerability.

"I'm sorry, Simon," Tamsen murmured, his voice heavy with regret. He gingerly laid Simon down on the ground, ensuring he was in a somewhat comfortable position before looking around, his senses on high alert.

The injury on Tamsen's shoulder throbbed relentlessly. With a glance around the deserted alleyway, he mustered all his strength and summoned his magic, a shimmering blue light enveloping his hand.

The arcane energy danced over his wound, knitting the torn flesh together. The process was excruciating, each suture-like sensation bringing a grimace to his face. Yet, Tamsen persevered, the urgency of his situation outweighing the pain.

As the last of the healing magic faded, Tamsen sagged against the alley wall, his breaths ragged. He closed his eyes, trying to compose himself and ignore the persistent ache that lingered beneath his skin. The air whispered around him, carrying distant sounds of the city- muffled footsteps, the occasional hushed conversation, and the faintest hint of music drifting from a nearby tavern.

Pushing himself away from the wall, Tamsen straightened his posture, his resolve hardening. He couldn't afford to dwell on the recent events; finding Abbie was paramount.

He could do this.

He would save his Abigail.

His mate.

Maybe if he found Jett, he'd find her too...

AS SIMON LAY UNCONSCIOUS in the dimly lit alleyway, a disturbance in the night air rippled around him. The faint glow that had once encased him waned, blending back into the shadows. The distant clatter of boots against the cobblestones grew louder, echoing ominously in the silent night.

A group of city guards rounded the corner, their armor gleaming in the feeble moonlight that filtered through the alleys. The leader, a stern-faced man with a hardened gaze, halted abruptly at the sight of Simon's prone form.

"What in the hell?" the guard captain muttered, his hand instinctively moving to the hilt of his sword. His eyes narrowed as he scrutinized the scene before him.

One of the guards pointed a trembling finger toward Simon, his voice quivering with a mixture of fear and suspicion. "Captain, look! There's something... strange about him."

The captain's gaze sharpened, noticing the telltale signs of forbidden magic lingering in the air. Arcane residue hung like an invisible shroud around Simon, a silent testimony to the illicit use of powers that were strictly forbidden within the city limits.

"By the Gods," the captain muttered, a grim realization dawning on him. "Arcane darkness..."

"You think he's the one behind the attack?" Another guard- a young woman who had yet to encounter the Arcane- piped up, her voice trembling.

The captain shook his head, his gaze never leaving Simon's seemingly lifeless body. "Can't be. There's no way a little squirt like this could have taken down those guards."

"So what's going on here, sir?" a third guard asked, his voice wary.

The captain was silent for a moment, contemplating the situation.

"We're going to take him back to the barracks," he finally decided, his tone leaving no room for argument. "I want to know where he found such blasphemous runes..."

"But Captain, the King said all werewolves should be killed on sight-"

"The King can go screw himself," the captain replied, his jaw set. "The old man already handed everything over to his heirs by now..."

"Speaking of, Prince Alexios is supposed to be visiting this afternoon..." The young woman said.

"Gods be damned," He sighed. "Why now of all times?!"

"H-he said he wanted to make sure we had enough resources in case of a werewolf attack, they've been after other villages..."

"Fine, just fine. We'll tell him about this when he arrives. Then it'll be his problem, not ours."

Without another word, the guards began to drag Simon's body down the alley. As they passed Tamsen's hidden figure, the captain paused, a look of suspicion crossing his features.

"Captain?" one of the guards asked, her voice wavering slightly.

The captain waved a hand dismissively.

"Just a chill, nothing more," he said, shaking his head. "Now come on, we've got work to do."

Tamsen stood, his body tense, his mind racing.

He had to get Simon out of there.

But he couldn't risk being caught, not while the city was still on high alert.

There had to be a way...

Simon's body was hoisted onto one of the guard's imposing Clydesdales, a beast of a horse that was the perfect steed for the job.

"Come on, move it!" The captain barked, urging his men to get a move on.

They rode out of the alley, their heads held high.

As the sounds of hooves against stones faded into the cold echo of the morning, Tamsen, once the leader of the pack, once the one who held them all together, once the one who would give anything for his friends...

He stood alone.

Abigail was gone, his pack was missing, and the only other person he cared about was taken from him.

Tears began to fall, his breath becoming ragged.

His heart shattered.

He had lost everything.

"Simon," he breathed, his voice barely a whisper.

Chapter Nineteen

When Simon came to, his eyes flew open, his body immediately tensing. His heart raced, the panic rising inside him. He was in an unfamiliar room, his body aching from head to toe. He tried to sit up, but he was bound, his wrists tied behind his back.

"What the..."

He squirmed, his hands twisting and pulling at the rope that bound him. All he could feel was the cold hard stone ground below, but he could smell the bitter scent of blood and leather lingering in the air.

"Fuck!!"

He heard the creak of a door opening, and he turned his head, his eyes wide.

"You're awake."

A deep laugh came from the darkness before him.

"When the guards told me there was a werewolf lurking around the streets of this city, at first, I called bullshit..."

A figure stepped forward.

The silver hair and deep crimson eyes could only mean one thing.

The Prince Alexios Caed himself.

"...then, when I saw you, I couldn't believe it. You look just like my little Naomi."

The mention of his sister made every hair stand on end.

He knew.

"Where is she? What have you done with her?" Simon growled.

"Relax, she's fine. For now. But you, you're a bit of a problem. Were-wolves are banned in the city, and not to mention, you used a little for-bidden magic there, didn't you?"

"Where is Abigail? Where is Naomi?!"

"Abigail?" Alex asked, tilting his head to the side. "It wouldn't happen to be an Abigail Drasa, wouldn't?"

"She's mine," Simon snapped. "I swear, I will rip your-"

Alex laughed. "Oh, Simon, you're not exactly in the position to be making demands."

"I swear to the Gods, if you've touched her-"

"I haven't, and I won't, unless she wants me to," Alex grinned. "I have a hard time turning down a girl's desires, when they ask me to please me..."

"You bastard!"

"You see, the thing is, I could kill you right now, and no one would question it. But that's no fun..." His eyes trailed the Betas form, and he licked his sharp fangs. "Or, I could bring you back to the castle with me. I could keep you. Your sister is my personal slave, after all, so you'd get plenty of time together."

"If you lay a hand on either of them, I'll kill you."

"Such a feisty wolf. I love it."

Simon growled, his eyes flashing gold.

Alex laughed.

"Guards! Bring him. I'm taking him home."

AFTER HOURS OF WANDERING the city, Tamsen's feet brought him back to the tavern, where it all had started.

But things had changed.

Everything was different.

His world was upside down. He stepped through the doorway, the familiar smells of alcohol and smoke filling his nostrils. None of it sank through to his foggy mind as he dragged himself further into the establishment.

There were people laughing, dancing, singing, drinking.

No one noticed the lone figure enter the room.

He was a shadow, a ghost.

His heart was empty, his soul crushed.

He made his way through the crowd, his steps slow and purposeful. He settled down into the seat, ordering a drink from the bartender. The liquor burned his throat, but he didn't care. He was numb, his body and mind detached. It was like he was floating, lost in the haze of his own despair.

Time went on, and bartender kept filling his glass. The hours passed, and the crowd thinned. Tamsen sat, staring into the distance.

He didn't move.

He couldn't.

"Did you hear that the Prince was in town?" Another patron- a middle-aged woman with a mess of curly grey hair and one too many glasses of honey-wine in her body- said as she nudged her friend.

"No, what happened?" Her friend asked curiously.

"Well, word on the street is, he captured a werewolf, and took him back to the castle with him."

"A werewolf?"

"Mhm, he's quite handsome, or so I've heard."

"A handsome werewolf, huh? Sounds like someone I'd want to get to know."

"Oh, don't be ridiculous. He's probably a monster."

"Or, maybe he's just misunderstood."

"Whatever you say. Now, enough about that, tell me about your date last night..."

Tamsen sat, his body rigid, his mind racing.

His grip tightened on the glass.

They were taking Simon to the castle?

"I'll meet you there, Simon," He whispered to his ale.

"Sir? Is everything alright?" The bartender asked, a worried expression on his face.

"Perfect. Everything is perfect," Tamsen muttered. "In fact, can I buy a round of drinks for everyone? My name's Tamsen."

"Are you sure?"

"Yes. I'm sure."

The patrons cheered, raising their glasses.

"To Tamsen! A true gentleman!"

Tamsen sat, the words of the two women echoing in his mind.

"A werewolf, huh? Sounds like someone I'd want to get to know."

"Or, maybe he's just misunderstood."

Maybe, just maybe, Abbie would understand...

And so, he drank.

He drank until his vision was blurry, and his mind was numb.

He drank until his thoughts were silenced, and the pain was gone.

He drank until the world around him faded, and he was alone, in the darkness.

And as he sank into the sweet embrace of oblivion, he knew that no matter what happened, he would always love her.

BY THE TIME HIS GLASS was empty for the tenth time, something flickered within him.

Something snapped.

A smile crept across his lips.

Maybe, it wouldn't be so bad that Simon was temporarily out of the picture. They were already planning to rescue Iris, and adding another rescuee wouldn't change things that much- *right?*

The thought sent a shiver down his spine, and his fingers twitched.

Maybe, just maybe, there was a way he could have Abigail all to himself.

And if there wasn't, well, he'd *find* a way.

He'd find a way to keep her away from Jett. He wasn't sure if Jett even had the thought of being her mate, but an idea like that was something he could crush- *eventually*. Either way, he might have to wait, wait for the perfect opportunity to get between them, but it would all happen in due time.

He'd take it slow.

Even if...

He swallowed thickly, hating himself for the thought.

I'll have to share her for now.

Because she was his, and nothing would change that.

Not even his friends.

Not even her.

Not even the Gods themselves.

She would be *his*, or he would die trying.

His smile widened.

And suddenly, everything was clear.

"You've had enough, sir."

"Nah, I'm good," He slurred, tapping his glass. "One more."

"I insist, please, allow me to escort you home."

"Ugh...Nah, I'm good. But thanks for the offer."

"Very well, but if you need anything, please don't hesitate to ask."

"Thanks, man."

With that, Tamsen slipped out the door.

The night was still young, and he had a plan.

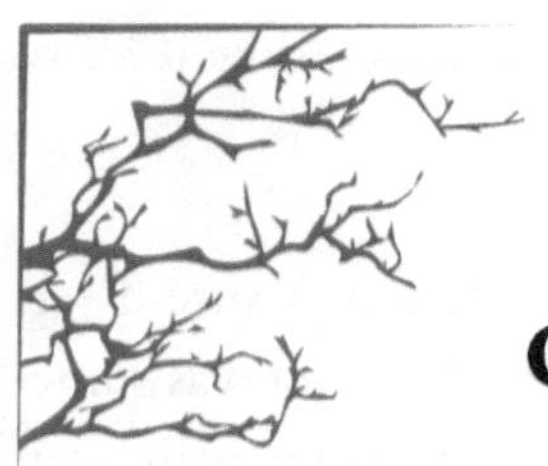

Chapter Twenty

Abbie's eyes fluttered open, the light streaming through the window waking her from her slumber. She sat up, rubbing her eyes, her gaze falling on Jett's sleeping form. He was sprawled across the bed, the blankets tangled around his legs, his face peaceful.

Her eyes drifted to his arms, the memory of his embrace still fresh in her mind. She could still feel the tingle of his touch on her skin, the heat of his kiss on her lips.

She didn't have to think about it for long, because a moment later, she felt Jett's soft lips on hers. He gently kissed her, his fingers brushing her hair away from her face.

"Good morning," he murmured, his voice thick with sleep.

"Morning," she said, her voice barely a whisper.

She wrapped her arms around him, pulling him closer, her body melting into his. She didn't care that they weren't much more than strangers, but she already felt such a connection within the group. She didn't care that the whole thing was crazy. All she cared about was this moment.

"Gods, I missed you," he said, his voice low and husky. His hands trailed along her neck, across her shoulders, all the way down to her wrists. "I just can't get enough..."

He kissed her deeply, his tongue slipping into her mouth, tasting her, exploring her. She moaned, her hands tangling in his hair, her body aching for him.

She didn't know why she felt so safe, so comforted by his presence. She had only known him for a short time, and yet, it was like her soul had always known him.

He kissed her neck, his teeth lightly scraping her skin. She shivered, the sensation sending a thrill through her.

"I'm so glad I met you," he whispered, his breath hot on her ear. "You weren't meant to be their mate, you were meant for *me*."

She moaned, her body aching for him. He gently pushed her onto her back, his lips never leaving hers. He pressed against her, his erection throbbing between her legs. She reached down, trying to be discreet as she touched herself, desperate for attention as he kissed every spot he could.

"Gods," he groaned, his hips bucking against her, his need growing.

"...shouldn't we...get going?" She tried to ask between hungry kisses, but she certainly didn't want him to stop.

"Don't worry, we'll get going soon enough. But for now, we've got plenty of time."

"Are you sure? I don't want us to get behind schedule-"

"I'm sure."

"But we need to-"

"Shhh," he said, his voice barely above a whisper. "Just let me enjoy this."

Abbie sighed, her body relaxing, her mind going blank as Jett's lips moved against hers. Between the heat of the passionate kisses and the feeling of his body pressed against her, she didn't even notice as Jett firmly pinned her wrists above her head.

She felt something rough graze her wrists and her eyes fluttered open, revealing Jett fixing her arms to the bedpost above her, using her own discarded dress as bindings.

"Hey," She protested, "What are you doing?"

"Something I've been dreaming of since the moment I saw you," He replied, a mischievous glint in his eyes.

Abbie tugged on the restraints, but they were tight. She was trapped.

"Jett," she whined, "Please...can I just..."

She squirmed, the desire to resume touching herself becoming insatiable.

"What's wrong, Darling?" He grinned beneath the morning-bedhead messy tassels of his dark hair. "You want more?"

His warm tongue dragged down her neck, leaving behind a trail of goosebumps. She shuddered beneath him, gasping when his teeth grazed her nipple. All the while, he worked to tighten the knot on the bedpost, ensuring there was no way she'd be able to rub without his permission.

"I w-want..." She whimpered, closing her eyes as her face blushed a deep red. "Please, Jett, you don't have to tie me..."

"Oh, but I think I do," he said, his lips trailing along her jaw. "Besides, didn't you say you'd do anything I wanted in exchange for my assistance on this mission?"

Abbie blushed, the memory of her words coming back to her.

"I guess so..."

"Good."

He kissed her deeply, his hands roaming her body, his fingers teasing her nipples, eliciting another breathy gasp from her.

"I'm going to make you beg," he said, his lips hovering over her ear. "I'm going to show you just how much I want you, all of you..."

"Please," she whispered, her body trembling.

"That's what I like to hear."

His hands slipped between her legs, his fingers teasing her folds. She moaned, her hips bucking against him, her body aching for him.

"Gods, you're wet," he groaned, his breath hot on her skin.

"Please," she whimpered, her body shaking.

"Tell me what you want."

"You," she gasped, her mind hazy.

"Beg for me," he commanded, his fingers circling her clit.

"Please," she begged, her voice a desperate plea. "Please, I need you."

"You need me?"

"Yes!"

He slid two fingers into her, curling them and hitting her g-spot, eliciting a cry from her.

"Please, Jett, I'm yours!"

"Good girl."

He thrust his fingers deeper into her, his thumb stroking her clit, her body writhing beneath him.

"I want to hear you scream," he growled, his free hand grabbing her throat.

"Gods, Jett, please, I'm yours," She whimpered, her eyes rolling back in pleasure. She could barely make a sound, the rhythm of the bed knocking against the wall overriding any other thought in her mind. Her legs already trembled with the desperation of an impending orgasm, and his dominance only sent her closer to the edge.

"Louder," he ordered, his grip on her throat tightening.

"Jett!" She screamed, her climax approaching.

"Come for me, Abbie."

He pumped his fingers into her, the heel of his palm grinding against her clit, her orgasm building with each thrust. She cried out, the ecstasy washing over her in waves.

"Good girl," he praised, his fingers never ceasing their relentless assault.

Her body quivered, her inner walls contracting around his fingers.

"Please, I'm yours, Jett," she repeated, her voice a ragged moan.

"That's right," he said, his eyes locking onto hers, his voice a deep, possessive whisper. "*Mine.*"

"I'm *yours,*" she breathed, her climax crashing over her. She gasped, her eyes rolling back, her body trembling as the aftershocks of her orgasm rippled through her.

He released her throat, his lips trailing along her neck, her body limp beneath him.

"Shhh," he said, his hands soothing her. "I'm not done with you yet."

She shivered, her nerves on fire, her need for him growing by the second.

"I need you," she begged, her voice a breathless plea.

"And I need you," he replied, his lips brushing hers.

"Please," she whimpered, her hips grinding against him, the evidence of his desire pressed against her.

"Please what?"

"Take me," she moaned, her voice barely a whisper.

He smirked, his expression dark and wicked.

"Gladly, Darling."

He positioned himself at her entrance, the tip of his cock teasing her. She bucked her hips, trying to take him, but he held back.

"Patience, my dear," he said, his eyes glinting.

"Please," she pleaded, her need growing by the second.

He made her wait, enjoying every moment of her desperate writhes beneath him. He took pride in watching her squirm- he hadn't indulged his sadistic side for far too long, and doing it with her...it just felt *right*. When he finally had his fill, he shoved his entire length into her, all the way down to the hilt.

He plunged into her, filling her, his hips thrusting as hard as he could manage, his cock slamming into her. She moaned, her hands tugging against the restraints, her body trembling.

"Oh, gods, Jett," she cried, her voice a hoarse moan.

"Fuck, Abbie," he growled, his pace frantic, his need evident.

"Gods, I'm yours," she moaned, her body rocking with each thrust.

"Mine," he grunted, his fingers digging into her hips.

She writhed beneath him, her climax approaching, her breath ragged.

"I'm yours," she breathed, her body quivering.

"Come for me, Abbie."

She cried out, her body convulsing, her inner walls contracting around him, the pleasure almost too much to bear.

He let out a primal roar, his body tensing, his cock pulsing inside her, her name on his lips.

He panted, his movements slowing as the two came down from the high of the moment. Eventually, he collapsed next to her. She nuzzled into him, barely able to move after the escapade- but a smile stuck on her lips.

"I love you, Abbie," He whispered.

Chapter Twenty One

The soft hues of dawn seeped through the curtains, casting a gentle glow on the serene figure of Abbie nestled in the sheets. Her long, cascading blonde locks spilled over the pillow, framing her delicate, pale face adorned with a sprinkle of freckles that danced across her cheeks like constellations in the night sky.

A tender smile brushed Jett's lips as he gazed upon her, his heart swelling with affection. The tranquility of her sleeping form was a portrait of ethereal beauty, an enchanting sight that stirred an overwhelming sense of adoration within him.

She was so beautiful, so perfect. He could watch her sleep all day.

Then, when loud, stumbling footsteps rang out from the hall, he decided to go investigate.

With utmost care not to disturb her peaceful rest, Jett gingerly untangled himself from the covers, the floor yielding silently beneath his cautious steps. He ventured into the hallway, his senses alert, seeking the origin of the intrusive footsteps that had disturbed the morning's tranquility.

His scrutiny fell upon Tamsen, the Alpha Werewolf, whose sun-kissed locks glinted under the faint light filtering through the windows. Tamsen bore an air of self-assurance, his demeanor marked by a confident swagger and a smug grin that hinted at mischief or worse.

Jett's patience wore thin, his eyes narrowing in suspicion, refusing to entertain Tamsen's deflection.

He knew that look.

"What did you do?"

Tamsen's smile faltered, his eyes widening at the sound of Jett's voice.

"How are you doing this morning, friend?"

"Cut the crap," Jett said, his voice low and dangerous. "What did you do?"

"Why, I haven't the faintest idea what you're talking about."

"I'm not stupid. You're not a morning person, and if you're smiling at this hour, I might as well assume the sky is falling momentarily-"

Tamsen hesitated for a moment.

Jett couldn't tell if he was just being coy or if he was conjuring a lie.

"Funny. You forgot about your little weapons sale, huh? Guy was pissed you didn't show to meet him. The city guards know we're here. One of the Caeds, even. Had to use magic. I'm fucking wound up, and I need to blow off some steam," He held up a palm, wiggling his blood-caked fingers. "Things got a little messy."

Jett's stomach dropped.

"You're a real piece of work, you know that?"

"And you're a liar," Tamsen smirked. "A liar, a thief, and a coward. Just like your father."

"Fuck off," Jett said, his voice barely a whisper.

"What was that?" Tamsen took a step forward, bristling at his tone. He was not a cruel Alpha, but he certainly wasn't going to tolerate the raven-shifter he'd so graciously adopted into their pack to try and start a fight. "If I'm not mistaken, I saw you at the market stuffing your jacket with stuff. It was for her, wasn't it?"

"She's none of your concern."

"Oh, really? Then why are you the one guarding her?"

"Tamsen, you're drunk. And you're making a scene."

"I'm not drunk. I'm just having a little fun. Don't worry, no one is watching."

"I can smell the alcohol on your breath."

"What did you steal, anyways?" He asked, stuffing his hands into his pockets as he tried to change the subject. "Anything good?"

"None of your business."

"Was it a necklace, or a ring? Did you get her a fancy dress? Some flowers? Chocolates? A bracelet?"

"It's none of your damn business," Jett growled.

"Ah, the silent treatment. My favorite."

"Leave me alone."

"Make me."

"You're insufferable."

"And you're an asshole. We're even."

"Look, I'm not going to argue with you, but please, just go away."

Tamsen nodded, pushing past him.

"Cool, I'm crashing here then."

His gaze fell upon the breakfast table, where the leftovers remained from his stolen-food haul.

"Looks delicious," He quipped, stealing a nibble of an uneaten pancake.

"You can't have any. It's mine."

"We're sharing it, remember?"

"No."

"Yes."

"Fine."

"*Excellent.*" Tamsen plopped down on the wooden chair, propping his legs up on the table. Jett clenched his jaw, glaring at the smug Alpha. "What?"

"You're the worst."

"Aw, I'm sorry. Am I cramping your style?"

His gaze fell on Jett's coat, hung neatly near the door. Another object, a stolen prize, dangled out of his pocket.

"What's that over there? Another trinket from your treasure hunting? Let me see-"

"N-nothing!" Jett asserted, immediately putting his coat on.

"Your Alpha commands you to be a good boy and tell me," Tamsen purred, earning a scoff from Jett. "Come on, don't be such a prude."

"When are we leaving?" Jett mumbled, fighting against the urge to fight back.

"We're staying in town for another night," Tamsen replied. "Main road is blocked by the Prince's caravan."

"Great."

"Yeah, great."

Jett stared at the ground, his heart pounding in his chest.

"I'll get packed," Jett answered. "You wouldn't happen to have any spare...rope or anything, right?"

"Why in the holy fuck would you need that?"

"Arts and crafts," Jett replied sarcastically. "Why else?"

"You can't..." His wolf bellowed from below, aching for another fight, but he was just about out of energy. And now, with Simon...

"She's not going to take another delay lightly," Jett argued. "...I think she's going to leave all of us, if we give her the chance. An ounce of prevention is worth a pound of cure."

Tamsen knew he would fight Jett for Abbie, but...

He couldn't lose another member of the pack over her.

For the first time, Tamsen conceded. His anger fizzled out like dying embers, and he simply sighed.

It seemed like sharing his prize would be the only option.

"Look, if you want to tie the poor girl up, you'll have to do it with your own damn shirt or something."

"That's not really my style."

"Who are you, and what did you do with Jett?"

"Nevermind," Jett huffed. "I'll figure something out."

"Fine, but if I see that girl walking around with rope burns on her wrists, I'm going to have to assume you're being a complete tool."

"Noted," Jett said, fighting back the urge to punch Tamsen in the face.

He knew the Alpha was just looking out for him, but damn, he didn't have to be such a dick about it.

Jett retreated back to his room, his thoughts racing. He knew he couldn't trust Abbie, and he had to keep her under control until he figured out what the hell was going on.

Part of him felt guilty- he knew just how much she wanted to find her sister. He knew that she had come to him to go along with the plan...

But it was too dangerous.

The Caeds would love another shot at capturing him. For years he had been a thorn in their side- constantly passing weapons to those most capable to use them, slowly empowering humans and werewolves alike to have a fighting chance against the monsters who held them down.

And Abigail wanted to go right to them. She'd put them all in danger, just because she wanted to rush the plan.

No, he couldn't let that happen. No matter how reckless or naive she was about the way of the world. She'd get taken in a heartbeat. Just like her sister had been.

He bristled, seething at the thought of what they'd do to her.

He had to protect her.

No matter what.

From the vampires, from the mages, and even from Simon...

He clenched his fists, his anger rising at the thought of the other wolf. He had no idea what was going on between the two of them, but whatever it was, it needed to stop. He didn't even question it when Tamsen had returned alone, and frankly, he was happy that he didn't have to see Simon. One less to worry about...

He wasn't going to lose her to just another wolf.

Never again.

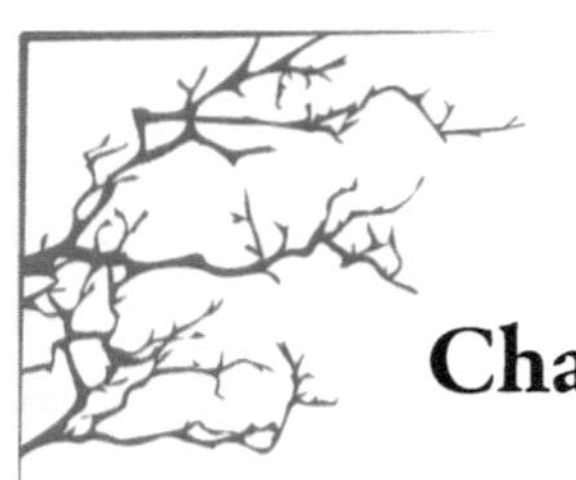

Chapter Twenty Two

His mind was made up. He'd tie her up, and he'd make sure that she wouldn't run. He couldn't bear the thought of losing her, or worse...

He had to keep her safe.

Abbie awoke, a splitting headache splitting through her skull. She groaned, rolling over to face the ceiling, the room spinning around her.

What the hell had happened last night?

She tried to move, but found that her arms and legs were restrained.

Panic immediately flooded through her veins, and her eyes snapped open.

The first thing she noticed was the rope.

Her wrists were bound to the bedpost, and her ankles tied together.

Her breath caught in her throat, her heart pounding furiously in her chest.

What the fuck is happening?! Where is Jett?!

Straining against the unforgiving ropes that bound her wrists, Abbie felt the constriction dig deeper into her skin with every futile attempt to break free. The intricate knot, a labyrinth of entwined fibers, seemed an impenetrable barrier to her freedom. A whimper escaped her lips as she surveyed the room with frantic desperation, her wide eyes darting around the unfamiliar space that enclosed her.

Nothing.

She was alone.

Had she done something wrong?

Was she being punished for something?

Or was this just part of the kinky shit Jett was into?

No, he wouldn't have left her.

Not like this.

He was an asshole, but he wasn't evil.

Right?

The conflict between her fear and lingering trust waged a battle within her conscience.

Time stretched mercilessly, each minute dragging like an eternity, amplifying the unnerving stillness until the haunting creak of the door shattered the oppressive silence. Tamsen's formidable figure breached the threshold, casting an ominous shadow across the room. Abbie's heart lurched in her chest at the sight, her voice trembling as she attempted to steady herself.

The tremor in her voice betrayed her growing anxiety, an unspoken plea for answers amidst the chaos that gripped her.

"Hello, Abbie," Tamsen replied, his tone veiled in an unsettling calmness that sent shivers down her spine. "Looks like you're in a bit of a bind there."

"W-what's going on? Where's Jett? What the hell are you doing to me?!"

"Calm down, you're fine. Jett's busy."

"Busy with what?!"

"Pack business."

"What am I doing here?! Why am I tied up?!"

"It's for your own good. Now shut up and be a good girl, will you?"

She squirmed beneath the bindings as a scowl fell upon her lips. The intricate knots only tightened around her wrists and ankles, the threads rough against her soft skin.

"Now, now, let's not be hasty-"

"I want Jett!"

"Tough."

"Please, Tamsen...Just tell me what's going on."

"I already did."

"Why won't you untie me?"

"Because Jett asked me not to. He said he thinks you're going to try to run away from us. It's not safe for you out there, and he's got some errands to run before we leave the city."

Abbie's frustration simmered beneath the surface, her voice tinged with a mix of anger and confusion that mirrored the turbulent emotions swirling within her. The abruptness of Jett's departure without a word of explanation felt like a betrayal, leaving her stranded in a whirlwind of unanswered questions.

"*Errands*? What kind of fucking errands?! And why didn't he wake me up?! You guys are the ones who wanted me to tag along, and now he's leaving me behind?!"

Tamsen's response dripped with an air of condescension, a trace of impatience evident in his retort.

"He's trying to protect you, stupid. If he'd told you where he was going, you would've wanted to go with him."

"Of course I would! Why wouldn't I?!"

"It's complicated," Tamsen replied vaguely, attempting to skirt around the heart of the matter.

"Bullshit!"

Tamsen's demeanor shifted slightly, his gaze fixated on her in a way that sent a shiver down her spine, an unsettling hunger lurking in his eyes.

"Abbie, please. I've brought you something to eat, and..." His voice trailed off, the unspoken implications lingering in the charged atmosphere between them. "I wanted to make sure you're still behaving yourself."

"I'm not hungry," Abbie retorted, her defiance evident in her refusal.

"You need to eat."

"No."

The standoff persisted, Tamsen's patience wearing thin as frustration flared between them.

"Why are you being so difficult?"

"Because I'm not going to let you or Jett get away with this!"

Tamsen's response was terse, a thinly veiled warning that underscored the escalating tension.

"Fine. If that's the way you want to play it."

"What's that supposed to mean?"

"It means you're acting like a brat."

The exchange crackled with animosity, each word a barb aimed to wound. Tension hung thick in the air as their verbal jousting intensified, a battle of wills fraught with underlying currents of unease and unspoken desires.

"*And* you're a tease. But you don't hear me complaining," Tamsen retorted, a smirk dancing on his lips, his words laced with a hint of veiled provocation.

"Fuck off."

"Don't be so cold. Just think about the fun we had last night."

"You're delusional. I've never done anything with you."

"Am I? I know you liked it. You couldn't stop moaning. Even after the others left, you were begging me for more. And more."

"Y-you're lying..."

"Am I? Because I can still hear the sounds of your voice in my head, crying out my name as you came over and over again."

Even if it was a lie, the way her face turned a deep shade of red, and she looked away muttering every curse under the sun.

"So, tell me...What were you thinking about, exactly? When I made you scream?"

"Fuck. You."

"You'll have to do better than that."

"Go to hell."

"I'm already there."

"Then I hope it burns."

"Oh, it does. But I can't help but wonder, what's going on in that pretty little head of yours? Are you remembering our kiss, or perhaps how it felt to have my hands on your body, touching and exploring every inch of your perfect skin?"

It was all things that he had wanted to do.

Things that had been just out of reach.

Alphas were used to getting their way. A game of hard-to-get was normally easily won, but Abigail had been different. She'd fallen for the others first, against the natural orders of everything, a prize that was forever beyond his grasp.

It was maddening.

And so was his cock, throbbing painfully as he stared at her exposed body.

The fact that Jett had tied her up was only making it worse.

He wanted nothing more than to bury himself deep inside her and take her, claim her as his own, make her beg for him.

He clenched his jaw, a wave of desire crashing through him.

Fuck.

This was torture.

How the hell was he supposed to be able to hold back now?

With her spread eagle and helpless, he could do anything he wanted to her.

Everything he wanted.

And he knew she wouldn't be able to resist him.

It was tempting.

He licked his lips, his heart racing in his chest.

Maybe, just maybe, if he played his cards right...

He could get exactly what he wanted.

What they both wanted.

His cock was aching, and it wouldn't take much to convince him to just take her right there and then. He knew he was playing a dangerous game, and he wasn't entirely sure how far he could go without pushing her over the edge.

"I can't decide if you're the best or worst thing that's ever happened to me," Tamsen growled, his wolf threatening to break loose.

"Go ahead," she whispered, her voice soft. "Try me."

His gaze drifted towards her, meeting hers. er eyes were burning with defiance, daring him to make a move.

Every bit of him wanted to take her, to teach her to regret taunting him, but despite everything- his eyes broke away from hers.

"I'm going to kiss you," He said, his voice barely a whisper.

She stiffened, her heart racing.

"N-no, you're not," She replied, her voice trembling. Each little teasing brush of his fingers along her body made her whimper, until he took her chin firmly into his hand, tilting her face up to his.

"I am," He whispered.

He leaned in closer, his lips mere inches away from hers.

"I am," He said, his breath hot against her ear.

He could feel the heat of her skin, and the quickness of her pulse.

His hand slid down her body, and he began to stroke her inner thigh, his touch making her gasp.

"And when I'm finished," He growled, "I'm going to untie you, and you're going to eat. Understand?"

"Y-yes," She whimpered.

He smiled, his lips brushing against hers.

"Good girl."

His tongue danced across her bottom lip, making her tremble.

"Do you want me to stop?" He purred, touching the tightened knots that bound her to the bed. "We could have a little fun first, before I let you out of these..."

"N-no," She stammered., her mind dizzy. Why did she feel the urge to obey him? His touch was hot, sending little shocks of pleasure through her. Every fiber in her body wanted to simply submit, to let the Alpha take her. "Don't stop..."

"Then let's make this easier, shall we?"

His fingers slipped inside her panties, his touch making her moan.

"That's a good girl," He said, his fingers teasing her clit.

"T-tamsen..." She gasped, her body arching against his touch.

"Mm, yes, my little princess? Tell me, what is it you want?"

"T-touch me," She breathed, her eyes fluttering closed.

"Oh, I intend to."

"P-please," She whimpered.

"Please what?"

"Please make me cum."

"Such a naughty girl."

He planted hot, wet kisses down her neck, nipping at her sensitive skin. She shuddered when his teeth grazed her nipple, where he spent a moment sucking gently on it. It felt so good she couldn't make a sound, simply opening her legs even more for him.

He could smell her arousal, and it made his heart quicken.

Tamsen moved lower, his stubble rough against her skin, his tongue tracing a line down the soft curves of her belly, before she could feel his hot breath on her clit.

"Please, Tamsen..." She begged, moving her hips.

"See, it doesn't take long for one to submit to an Alpha..." A devilish smile spread across his lips, and his blue eyes glanced up and met hers. "I should reward you for coming to your senses."

He tore his gaze from here, his attention returning to the task at hand.

His warm lips moved in, a sloppy kiss placed on her quivering clit. She gasped, almost pulling away at first. Her senses were flooded, electricity of pleasure erupting from every spot he licked. Even with the restraints, his strong hands held her tightly for good measure.

Finally, when she was just about to get to the edge, he pulled away, his lips releasing her clit with a little *pop*.

"Do you want me to keep going?"

"Yes," She moaned, her eyes closing.

"Beg for it," He whispered, his voice low and husky.

"P-please," She whimpered, her body trembling with pleasure. "Tamsen, I want you so much..."

He hesitated for a long moment, before he sighed, pulling away. Abbie almost begged him to start again, but then, the door opened with a creak, and Jett entered the room.

"What the fuck are you doing here?" He growled.

Tamsen grinned, his fingers still inside her.

"Just having a little fun," He said, his eyes darkening with lust. "You can join us, if you'd like."

"Like hell I will," He growled.

"Come on, don't be like that," Tamsen purred, his thumb rubbing her clit. His mind was still clouded with the liquor, and he didn't want Jett to ruin the mood. Jett clenched his jaw, his eyes flashing with anger. "Don't be a pussy. You know you want her."

Jett hesitated, his mind torn.

He could still remember how good it had felt when he'd kissed her. How soft her lips had been. How she had moaned, her body trembling in pleasure.

And the thought of Tamsen's hands on her body, touching and caressing her...

His cock twitched, a low growl escaping his lips.

"See? You want her. She wants you. So come on, stop being such a pussy and fuck her."

"I'll think about it," He grunted.

"Suit yourself."

Jett's gaze fell upon Abbie, and he froze, his eyes widening.

She was staring at him, her expression unreadable.

"H-hi," He stammered.

"Hey," She whispered.

"How cute," Tamsen chuckled. "Aren't you two adorable?"

"Shut up," Jett hissed.

"Don't be like that," Tamsen purred, his fingers working her clit. "I don't know what you're waiting for."

"T-tamsen..." She whimpered. She didn't want to sound like a slut, especially now that it felt like she had an audience. How could she moan for Tamsen when Jett was right there- or vice versa?

"Do you want him to fuck you?" Tamsen purred, his voice husky. "Or do you want me? Pick your poison, Princess."

"J-jett..." She whimpered, her hips rocking against Tamsen's hand. "Oh, Tamsen..."

"Is that a yes, or a no?"

In a lust-fuelled haze, she blurted out the first thing on her mind. *The only thing on her mind.*

"Both."

There was a moment of stunned silence, and Tamsen even stopped moving momentarily. Then, Tamsen chuckled, giving Abbie a playful smack on the ass. She yelped, muttering curses at him as she squirmed, her pleasure more than evident in the slickness between her legs.

"You know," Jett said, his eyes darkening with lust. "There's a few hours to kill before the caravan is out of the way...we could take turns fucking her."

"Sounds like a plan to me," Tamsen purred, a devilish smile tugging at the corners of his lips.

"I've never...been with two guys at the same time before," She whispered, unsure of herself. "I don't know if I can..."

"Well," Tamsen smirked. "Today's your lucky day."

He leaned in close, his breath hot against her ear.

"Because you're ours."

IN A MIX OF TAVERN-induced arousal and the frustration that he was the Alpha and hadn't been first, Tamsen swiftly popped open the buttons to his tunic and removed his clothes in the blink of an eye.

Abbie's mouth went dry, her eyes raking over her naked body.

Gods, he was gorgeous.

Tamsen sauntered over to the bed, a cocky smirk on his lips.

"See, it's not that hard to share," He mused, while Abbie's jaw was still dropped from the sight of him naked.

"I'll share her with you, but I get to keep her," Jett stated, his eyes narrowing.

"None of that yet," Tamsen said, his smile widening. "Business first. I'll take her from behind."

"No."

"You've got the front covered," Tamsen shrugged, before positioning himself between her legs, his hands trailing along her thighs.

"Fuck off," Jett hissed, his tone icy.

"I'm already fucking her," Tamsen quipped, his gaze never leaving Abbie's.

Abbie's eyes widened, her cheeks flushed, her body trembling.

"Tamsen, please," Abbie breathed, her voice a shaky whisper. "I want you..."

"You're begging the wrong wolf, sweetheart," he replied, his voice husky. "You don't even know what you're asking for."

"Fuck off," Jett growled, his eyes flashing with rage.

"Jett, it's okay," Abbie pleaded, her voice soft. "Just let him..."

Her words trailed off as Tamsen rubbed the tip of his thick cock against her, teasing her gently.

"Oh, gods," she moaned, her hands tugging against the restraints, her back arching.

"That's it," Tamsen purred, his breath hot on her skin.

"Please," she panted, her body trembling.

Jett glared at him, his teeth clenched, his jaw set. He stripped quickly, a drive of jealousy washing over him, his movements jagged as he watched the duo.

Abbie writhed beneath Tamsen, her body aching for release. Jett couldn't stand to hear her moan for *him*, of all people, so he did what he could to quiet her. He took a fist full of her long hair, and in a swift thrust, he plunged his throbbing cock into her mouth.

She gagged, her eyes watering as it touched the back of her throat.

"Fuck, Abbie," he grunted, his hips thrusting, his cock sliding in and out of her mouth.

"Yeah, that's it," Tamsen crooned. "You're so good at this..."

Abbie cried out, her orgasm building, her body quivering.

"That's right," Tamsen said, his lips grazing her ear. "Come for me, Abbie. It'll make things easier for what comes next."

She moaned, the sound muffled by Jett's cock, her body trembling.

"I'm not stopping till I'm satisfied, Abbie," Jett groaned, his eyes locked onto hers.

"That's it," Tamsen murmured, his pace quickening, his lips trailing along her neck.

Jett gripped her hair tighter, his cock throbbing, his hips thrusting harder wih each passing moment. She felt Tamsen teasing her entrance, preparing her for a breeding by the Alpha.

"Oh, fuck," she moaned around the mouthful, the pleasure almost too much to bear.

Tamsen pushed into her, filling her, his cock stretching her.

"Gods, you're tight," he grunted, his grip on her hips bruising.

Abbie whimpered, her body writhing, the feeling of being so full driving her wild.

"Fuck, you feel good," Jett growled, his hips bucking, his cock slamming into her mouth. She gagged, her eyes rolling back, her body trembling.

"That's right, baby," Tamsen said, his breath hot on her skin. "You take my cock like a good girl."

Abbie's eyes fluttered open, her gaze locking onto Jett's.

"Gods, you're taking us both," Jett groaned, his eyes dark with lust. "Such a natural..."

Tamsen grunted, his hips thrusting, his cock slamming into her, her inner walls milking him. Abbie writhed, the pleasure building, her body aching for release. She was overwhelmed with the sensations, every inch of her submitting to the dominant aura of the two men who desired her so much.

"Don't you dare stop," Jett growled, his grip on her hair tightening.

"Make me come, baby," Tamsen panted, his voice thick with desire.

Abbie's eyes squeezed shut, her body quivering, the ecstasy washing over her.

"Yes," Jett hissed, his hips bucking, his cock throbbing.

"Fuck, Abbie," Tamsen grunted, his voice a low, animalistic growl.

Abbie cried out, her climax crashing over her, her body shuddering, her muscles tensing.

"Gods, you're perfect," Jett moaned, his eyes never leaving hers.

Tamsen thrust into her, his cock pulsing inside her, filling her with his seed.

` "Shit, Abbie," Jett grunted, his body quivering. "You're amazing..."

Abbie whimpered, her hips jerking, her body trembling.

Jett roared, his hips bucking, his cock twitching, spilling his seed into her mouth.

"That's a good girl," he purred, his voice husky.

"Mm, fuck, that was good," Tamsen breathed, his chest heaving.

"I've never..." Abbie mumbled, her voice hoarse as Jett pulled out of her mouth.

"Yeah, it's something you'll learn to love," Tamsen smirked, his eyes glinting. "Being shared."

Jett pulled out, and a few droplets of his cum fell onto her breasts, and her nipples stiffened from the sensation. She gasped, her heart skipping a beat.

"Gods, I can't believe you're mine," Jett murmured, his gaze locked onto hers.

"Mine too," Tamsen quipped, a smirk crossing his face.

"Mine first," Jett snapped.

"We'll see," Tamsen mused, his tone icy.

Jett untied her hands, and she immediately wrapped her arms around his neck, burying her face in his chest. He left one of the knots around her ankle though- an assurance that she wouldn't get any ideas in the middle of the night.

He lay down beside her, his arm wrapped around her.

"It's late," he said, his voice low.

"Yeah, I guess we should go to sleep," she whispered, her eyes closed.

"Goodnight, Darling."

"Night, Jett."

"Sleep well."

"You too."

She was asleep in minutes, and Jett soon followed, his breathing soft and steady. Tamsen lay awake, staring at the ceiling, a frown etched into his face.

What was he going to do about Jett?

Chapter Twenty Three

Tamsen, with his commanding presence softened in the dim light, held Abbie close to him, their forms entwined in a protective embrace- after he'd gotten the opportunity to wiggle himself between her and Jett... despite his distaste for sleeping next to his *not-exactly-friendly* friend.

His blonde locks framed his angular features, accentuating his striking blue eyes that glimmered with a tenderness reserved only for her. The contours of his athletic physique provided a sense of security as he sheltered her from the uncertainties that loomed outside the inn's walls.

Abbie leaned into Tamsen's comforting embrace. Her blue eyes, once filled with apprehension, now held a glimmer of trust as she allowed herself to bask in the fleeting solace of his presence. Despite the circumstances that had brought them together- her captivity by these enigmatic men- there was an undeniable pull, a mysterious allure that made her heart flutter in conflicting emotions.

Realizing Tamsen's interferance in their sleeping position, Jett untangled himself from the trio. He stood and dressed himself, slipping his jacket over his shoulders.

He heard the soft jingle from his pocket, and in a moment of early-morning haziness, he'd almost forgotten about the stolen object.

His fingers gripped the smooth leather, and he held it up in the morning light.

The collar, fashioned with meticulous craftsmanship, was a testament to the skills of a master leatherworker. Its foundation was supple yet durable leather, dyed a deep, rich mahogany that gleamed under the gentle caress of sunlight. Delicate etchings adorned its surface, intricate patterns of intertwining vines and blossoming roses, each detail meticulously hand-tooled.

At its center rested a finely wrought emblem, a shining silver medallion shaped like a stylized paw print. The metalwork was exquisite, the paw's lines so finely etched that they seemed to pulse with life, catching the light and casting shimmering reflections across the room. Tiny, twinkling gemstones were embedded within the paw's design, each one a different shade of vibrant hues- a sapphire, an emerald, a ruby, and an amethyst- forming a captivating mosaic within the silver.

A deep blush fell across his face as he glanced back at Abbie.

It would look so good on her.

He hadn't wanted to give her two gifts in one day, but he'd been hoping to show it to her before Tamsen got in the way...

Ugh.

He didn't even want to think about the Alpha's hands on her.

Jett shoved the collar back into his pocket, reserving the toy for another day. He tried to collect himself- washing his face gently in the washbasin before fretting over his hair in the mirror. Eventually, he took to sitting in front of the window, his mind too uneasy to bother prepping any breakfast.

Then, his keen eyes caught a glimpse through the window- a telltale sign that the Prince's caravan had finally moved, clearing the path for their escape. Without a moment's hesitation, Jett abruptly stirred, a sense of urgency igniting within him.

"Get up," Jett's voice was terse, cutting through the quietude of the room. His abrupt awakening disrupted the tranquil moment, jolting both Abbie and Tamsen from their brief respite.

Tamsen's grip on Abbie loosened as he glanced towards Jett. Abbie stirred from her drowsy state, her gaze shifting from Tamsen to Jett, a ripple of confusion marring her features.

"What's happening?" Abbie's voice was laced with concern as she tried to make sense of the sudden change.

"The caravan has moved," Jett explained, his tone brusque yet focused. "It's our chance to leave unnoticed. Where's Simon?"

"He went ahead of us," Tamsen replied nonchalantly. "He's probably already at the castle by now, waiting for us."

"Wait, you didn't mention this before? I thought he was just mad at me," Jett replied, bewildered at the sudden revelation that the third pack member wouldn't be joining them.

"He is mad at you," Tamsen shrugged, rising to his feet and reaching out to help Abbie. Jett's keen eyes followed their movements, a hint of impatience lingering in his gaze as he untied her.

"Now, don't get any ideas of running," Tamsen said, his voice low as his teeth grazed her ear. "You don't want to find out what happens when my wolf gets angry..."

She blushed, a shiver running down her spine.

"N-no sir," She said, her heart thumping as she went along with his game.

Although Jett wasn't enjoying whatever Tamsen was playing.

"Let's move," Jett urged, gesturing towards the door.

Tamsen led the way, holding the door ajar as Abbie followed close behind. Jett trailed a short distance away, keeping a close watch for any signs of danger.

As they slipped through the door, the brisk morning air greeted them, a sense of exhilaration mingling with the apprehension of their escape. As they approached the edge of the village, a glimmer of the rising sun illuminated their path, guiding their footsteps as they hastened towards the treeline.

"About tying you up and all that..." Tamsen whispered into Abbie's ear, his breath warm on her neck. "I'm sorry, but I had to. And I'll have to do it tonight, too, just for good measure."

"Sure you did," She scoffed. Tamsen chuckled as he caught sight of the flustered blush that crossed her cheeks. "Absolutely imperative to the plan, was it now?"

"Positively sure," He replied, his hand trailing down her back. "Just as sure as I am about how much I want you."

A faint rustling in the trees caught their attention, prompting a moment of caution as they slowed their pace. Abbie glanced towards Tamsen, a ripple of anxiety flashing across her features.

"Should we keep going?" Abbie whispered, her voice trembling slightly.

"We need to get out of the open," Tamsen reassured, his tone steady. "Get to the horses, we mount up, make our way along the outskirts of the Caedwyn castle. We're going to the dungeons first. Abbie will be our distraction, like we planned, and Jett- you can use one of your blades. Try and find the Princes. Kill the younger one first."

"And I'll go and look for my father after I find Iris. I'll see if they have him. If not, he could still be in the village, and I'm not leaving without him. Not this time."

Tamsen nodded, "We'll split up. Jett and I will search the castle for any signs of your father. We'll meet back here when we're done."

"What if they capture us?" Abbie's voice quivered with uncertainty.

"They won't," Tamsen stated with conviction, his gaze piercing. "They don't know we're coming."

A faint breeze swept through the air, carrying with it the scent of impending danger. Jett's ears pricked up, detecting the slightest hint of movement nearby. He turned, his gaze narrowing as he searched the darkness for any signs of the source. A subtle rustle in the underbrush caught his attention, alerting him to the presence of another being lurking in the shadows.

"Trouble's headed our way," Jett warned, his voice low.

Tamsen's body tensed, his posture shifting into a defensive stance. His fingers twitched, the urge to shift into a wolf growing stronger by the second.

But he couldn't.

He couldn't trust his wolf not to hurt Abigail.

Abbie's wide, alert eyes frantically scanned their surroundings, her pupils dilated from the surge of adrenaline flooding her system. The rush made every detail around her hyper-vivid, from the flickering shadows to the faint rustling of leaves in the wind.

"What should we do?" She whispered, her voice barely audible.

Jett remained silent, his expression unreadable as he continued to scan their surroundings.

Then-

Crack!

Along with the sound, a putrid tang of magic hung in the air, heralding imminent danger. It struck Jett's chest, causing him to stagger, breath stolen, words trapped. A chilling metallic taste flooded his mouth as the world tilted, forcing him to his knees.

"No!"

"Jett!"

His vision blurred, but he could make out the faint outlines of Tamsen and Abbie. They rushed to his side, their voices echoing in his ears.

He was fading.

He could feel his life draining away, and there was nothing he could do to stop it.

The last thing he saw was the image of Tamsen and Abbie reaching out to him, their faces etched with concern and sorrow.

Then, everything went black.

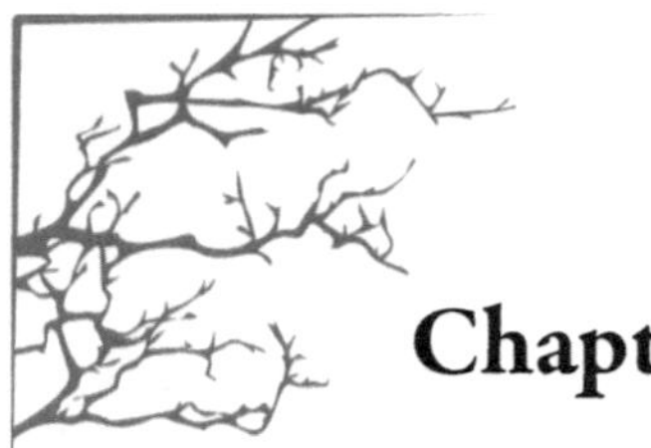

Chapter Twenty Four

They mages had found them.

Abbie and Tamsen exchanged glances, the weight of the situation settling on them like a heavy cloak. They were outnumbered and outmatched. There was no way they could fight their way out of this.

"We need to go," Tamsen's voice was calm, but the urgency was clear. "Now."

Abbie nodded, her eyes wide with fear.

"What about Jett?"

Tamsen grimaced, his gaze lingering on the limp body of his friend. The part of him that felt drawn to duty, that felt the need to protect his pack above all else, that part of him howled in agony. He couldn't even look at him anymore, tearing his gaze away as he felt his throat burn.

"There's nothing we can do for him," Tamsen replied, his voice heavy with grief. "We have to leave him."

But part of him...

Part of him, deep down in the fucked-up recesses of his mind, bellowed a bitter laugh. A laugh he'd never let Abbie hear, for it would destroy everything that he had worked so hard to build with her.

His problem had just solved itself.

He had her all to himself now.

Abbie's breath hitched in her throat, tears welling in her eyes. She knew Tamsen was right, but it didn't make the reality any less painful. Tamsen gently grasped her hand, his touch gentle yet reassuring.

"Come on," he murmured, pulling her towards the woods. "We need to get out of here before the rest of the mages arrive."

They ran, the trees and brush whipping past them in a blur. They had to put as much distance between them and the mages as possible. They had to survive.

They had no choice.

As they fled, the faint echoes of the mages' pursuit rang out behind them, reminding them that the battle had only just begun.

THE SUN BEGAN TO RISE, its rays illuminating the forest in a golden glow. Birds sang, and the sound of the breeze rustling the leaves was the only noise.

The mages were nowhere in sight.

Each step felt like an effort as Tamsen slowed to a halt, his chest heaving with exertion. Abbie, her legs protesting from the demanding journey, managed to catch up, her gaze meeting Tamsen's in a fleeting exchange before they pressed on, a wary glance cast over their shoulders, vigilant for any sign of pursuit.

The towering trees loomed like ancient sentinels, their thick foliage casting shifting shadows that played tricks on their vision, making navigation a challenge.

"We're almost there," Tamsen murmured, his voice a mere whisper that barely carried through the stillness of the forest. "Just a little further."

Abbie nodded, her eyes fixed on the path ahead, though her weariness threatened to overpower her senses. With each step, she struggled against the fatigue that threatened to consume her, her muscles protesting from the relentless trek.

Gradually, the dense woodland began to relent, the trees parting to allow a soft cascade of sunlight to filter through. The forest floor transformed, the softness of moss and the lushness of verdant grass offering a stark contrast to the unforgiving terrain they had traversed moments before.

She had to.

Abbie could feel her exhaustion catching up with her, the events of the previous day weighing heavily on her mind. Her body ached, and her eyelids threatened to close.

Abruptly, Tamsen's grip on her tightened, his sudden stillness pulling her attention. His eyes fixated on something in the distance, and Abbie followed his gaze.

"What is it?" Abbie whispered, following his gaze.

She gasped.

There, in the clearing, was a huge, imposing structure.

The castle.

"We made it," Tamsen breathed, his voice full of relief. "We're home."

Abbie stared at the castle in awe, taking in its impressive size and beauty.

So close now, Iris. Just hang on a little longer.

"We should keep moving," Tamsen murmured, glancing over his shoulder. "It's not safe to stay here for too long."

Abbie nodded, steeling her resolve.

She could do this.

She had to.

For Iris.

As they crept towards the castle, the sound of voices reached their ears.

Abbie's heart sank.

"Someone's coming," she whispered, her voice trembling slightly.

"Hide!" Tamsen hissed, pulling her behind a tree.

They waited, their bodies pressed against the rough bark. They could hear the voices getting closer, and their hearts pounded in their chests.

The sound of footsteps reached their ears, and they held their breath, waiting for the danger to pass.

"There's no sign of the wolves." A man's voice rang out.

"They must have gone in a different direction," another voice replied.

"Well, we can't let them get away," the first man said, his tone urgent. "They're a threat to the crown. They have to be dealt with."

Abbie's breath caught in her throat. The men were talking about them.

"Come on," Tamsen murmured, motioning for Abbie to follow him.

They slipped through the trees, keeping out of sight. The voices faded into the distance, and Abbie let out a sigh of relief.

"We're not out of the woods yet," Tamsen whispered, his gaze darting around the area.

"I know," Abbie replied, her voice barely audible. "But we're so close. We can't give up now.".

"Let's go," he whispered, pulling Abbie along with him.

The castle was within reach. They could do this.

Tamsen could feel his adrenaline pumping. The time was drawing near. His plan was simple, yet effective. All they had to do was get inside, free the prisoners, set the distraction fire, and find Abbie's sister and father. Then, once they were all free, he could challenge the king and take what was rightfully his.

"You ready?"

Abbie nodded, her gaze filled with determination.

"I'm ready."

THANKS FOR READING!

THANK YOU SO MUCH FOR taking the time out of your day to check out my rambling writings! I'm really excited to be able to share this series, that has been my escape for the last year, with you all. I hope you enjoyed it, and you had as much fun in the world as I did. If there are comments or feedback you'd like to give, I would be more than happy to take ideas- you might even inspire a new scene!

I hope you have a beautiful day, you wonderful human. :)

ABOUT THE AUTHOR:

A RISING STAR IN THE realms of Paranormal Romance (PNR) and Dark Fantasy, my goal is to tales that immerse readers in worlds where magic crackles in the air and passion ignites the pages. It's nice when there's a little heat in there, too, am I right? Known for crafting stories that are as spicy as they are enchanting, I infuse my narratives with a blend of supernatural allure and raw intensity that leaves readers spellbound.

For me, characters are key, and I like being able to have a narrative that's beyond just the sex. I'm usually listening to my favorite songs I enjoyed as a teen while I'm in Starbucks working on my next chapter. In addition to crafting otherworldly stories, I proudly embrace the role of a devoted cat mom to two adorable kittens who bring joy and mischief into my life. Alongside these furry companions, a majestic bearded dragon named Roxie holds court, lending an air of ancient wisdom and quiet companionship to my writing sanctuary.

With four enthralling books already penned and the eagerly anticipated fifth standalone installment in progress, I invite readers on a journey with me (your friendly caffienated mess of a tour guide) through realms where darkness and desire intertwine, where the extraordinary becomes the norm, and where love and danger collide in a symphony of thrilling escapades.

Amidst my literary endeavors, I proudly champion the mantra that disability is not a limitation but a source of strength. It's a reminder to myself and others that barriers are meant to be shattered, and the power within us transcends any societal confines. This belief infuses my work with resilience, authenticity, and a celebration of diversity that echoes throughout my stories.

If nothing else is ever taken from my career in writing, I want readers to see the characters grow and evolve. I want them to see the struggles, the trials and tribulations of life, all while holding out for that someone who has just the right hot stuff for you. While frustrating, adorable and a little addictive, I want their romantic journey to stand as a testament to the resilience of the human spirit, sending a resounding message to never let anyone diminish the strength found within ourselves.

CLICK HERE TO SIGN up for my email list! Be the first to know about new releases, ARC signups, events, giveaways, and more!

https://mailchi.mp/92625d7a5d78/ellelacerta

Other Books:

All of my books are available in Kindle Unlimited.
Book One: Contract Of The Crown
https://www.amazon.com/dp/B0CNTXVR6F
Book Two: Punished By The Prince
https://www.amazon.com/dp/B0CP194M4Y

Other Books